The
Heart
of the
Matter

Deanna Lynn Sletten

The Heart of the Matter
A Novel

Copyright 2025 © Deanna Lynn Sletten

ISBN–13: 978-1-941212-86-8

Cover Designer: Deborah Bradseth

Novels by

Deanna Lynn Stetten

HISTORICAL

The Last Lady of the Silver Screen
Mrs. Winchester's Biographer
The Secrets We Carry
The Ones We Leave Behind
The Women of Great Heron Lake
Miss Etta
Night Music
Finding Libbie

WOMEN'S FICTION

The Lifestyle
Christmas at Mountain View Lodge
The Christmas Charm
One Wrong Turn
Maggie's Turn
Summer of the Loon
Memories
Sara's Promise

MURDER/MYSTERY

Rachel Emery Series
The Truth About Rachel
Death Becomes You
All the Pretty Girls

ROMANCE

Destination Wedding

Lake Harriet Series
Under the Apple Blossoms
Chasing Bailey
As the Snow Fell
Walking Sam

Kiss a Cowboy Series
Kiss a Cowboy
A Kiss for Colt
Kissing Carly

YOUNG ADULT

Outlaw Heroes

The
Heart
of the
Matter

Chapter One

Marsha

Marsha Winslow sat at her dressing table, applying the finishing touches to her make-up. She studied her face and neck, lightly tracing her fingertips over her pale skin. At forty-five years old, her skin still looked smooth. Despite growing up in southern California, where her generation liberally bathed in the sun, she'd managed to protect her skin in her older, wiser years, and the damage didn't show yet. Still, she knew she didn't look like a dewy-fresh twenty-year-old. She was long past that.

Marsha shook out her shoulder-length dark brown hair to loosen the curl she'd meticulously added with a curling iron earlier. She liked having a little body to her hair but not a tight curl. Once her make-up and hair were finished, she added the finishing touch. Marsha lifted the gold heart necklace from its spot on her dressing table and carefully clasped it around her neck. The diamonds on the pendant sparkled in the light and made Marsha smile. Her husband of twenty years, Craig, had given her this necklace on their fifteenth anniversary, telling her she was the keeper of his heart. She absolutely cherished it.

"I'll be gone for only three days," Craig said, stepping out of the bathroom attached to their bedroom. His hand lovingly caressed Marsha's shoulder as he passed her on his way to the closet. Craig was seven years her senior and had gained a bit of weight lately, but he still cut a fine figure in a three-piece suit. He continued to speak as he tied his silk tie and slipped on his vest. "I just want to check in at the Monterey office so they don't think I've forgotten them," he said, buttoning up his vest. After putting on his suit jacket, he slid his feet into polished black shoes.

Marsha stood and walked over to him, looking up into his warm brown eyes. "I'm sure they know you haven't forgotten them," she said, grinning. She reached up and straightened the knot in his tie. "But it's always good to make an appearance."

Craig smiled back at her. "I'm sure they could easily forget me. You, however, are unforgettable." He kissed her sweetly on the lips, then turned to retrieve his overcoat from the closet.

"It's seventy-eight degrees outside," Marsha told him, stepping into the dark blue heels that matched her flowing blue and cream dress. "A coat isn't necessary."

"It's necessary in Monterey," he said.

"That's true." Marsha checked the contents of her husband's suitcase that lay open on the bed. "Do you have everything you need?"

"I think so," he said, giving the contents a cursory look.

"You must plan on golfing while you're there." Marsha had noted the cotton trousers and polo shirt in his bag.

"I'm hoping to get on the course tomorrow afternoon if I can," he said. "It's always a good way to relax and talk to the office manager. It's more casual that way."

Marsha nodded. She knew her husband conducted a lot of his business on golf courses.

Craig snapped the suitcase shut and lifted it off the bed. When he turned, he smiled again at his wife. "You look lovely today."

"Thank you." She was always grateful for the way Craig noticed and complimented her. After twenty years of marriage, their relationship hadn't dimmed. Craig always remembered important dates and was very attentive.

"How is the gallery doing?" he asked.

"Wonderfully," Marsha said. "Tourist season is all year round in California, thank goodness. We've sold a few very nice pieces lately. You should see the new sculpture Marco brought in. It's made of granite, and it's gorgeous."

"Sounds nice," Craig said. They walked together down the hallway toward the front door. Their lovely home in Palos Verdes sat on a cliff with an expansive view of the ocean. On the way to the door, they passed several rooms with large windows displaying breathtaking views.

Craig gave Marsha a kiss before opening the front door. "I can't wait to go on our anniversary cruise," he said softly. "Twenty years. It's gone by so quickly."

"Too quickly," Marsha said, leaning into him. "It'll be fun though. I can't wait."

"I'll see you in a few days." Craig kissed her again and then walked to his car in their driveway. The strands of silver that ran through his dark hair glistened in the sunshine as he put his suitcase in the back seat of his Mercedes EQS SUV and then slid in behind the wheel. With one last wave, his car drove away down their driveway and then through the neighborhood.

Marsha sighed, closed the door, and walked into the

kitchen for a second cup of coffee. Standing at the windows in the dining room, she enjoyed the view of the deep blue water. Their yard was large and lush with flowering hedges and small hidden alcoves. One held a swinging bench. Another private spot had a table and chairs where they sometimes enjoyed their morning coffee on weekends. They had a pool that sat under a large pergola and a back patio with an outdoor kitchen. She knew she was lucky to live this amazing life with a man who adored her and a job she loved. Despite never having been blessed with children—which Marsha would have loved to have experienced—their marriage was strong. And she couldn't wait until the end of the month when they'd celebrate their time together on a beautiful Caribbean cruise.

With one last sip of coffee, she grabbed her purse and headed out the door to her art gallery.

* * *

As Marsha drove the short distance inland from the coast to her art gallery at the lovely Promenade PV, she saw the huge billboard with her husband's handsome face advertising his business. She smiled. Craig Winslow Insurance Agency, it read, in large, red letters. He'd paid for two large billboards—this one and one on Highway One north. Every time Marsha drove past them, they made her smile.

Craig had started his first agency in Torrance a few years before she'd met him, and together, they'd worked hard—he as the agent and she as the office manager—and expanded to own offices in Malibu and Monterey. Years of hard work had paid off, and they'd purchased their dream home in Palos Verdes. Marsha had also been able to start Coastal Charm Gallery with her long-time best friend from college, Kristen. Her dear friend had been introduced to Craig's brother, Jeffery, by Marsha years ago and the two were happily married now. So together, Marsha and Kristi had opened a prestigious little art gallery which, over the past five years, had flourished.

Unlocking the glass door to the gallery, Marsha walked toward the back room to flip on the lights. She stopped for a moment to admire the smooth granite sculpture in the glass case that Marco had recently brought in. It was beautiful. She knew that one of their high-end clients would snatch it up as quickly as possible, and she wanted to enjoy it while it was here.

Locking her purse in the bottom desk drawer in the back, she snapped on the lights and headed up front again, walking around the glass cases displaying artwork.

"Good morning," Kristi chirped as she entered the front door. "It's such a beautiful day outside."

"Good morning," Marsha greeted her. She smiled at her energetic friend. Kristi was a petite ball of energy with short blond hair and bright blue eyes. Marsha hadn't a clue how Kristi kept up with her two young children, the art gallery, and her husband and still be bubbly every morning. But it was one of the reasons she loved her so much. "Yes. It is. Hopefully, we'll have plenty of people walking around the Promenade today, looking for gifts."

Kristi went to the back room to put away her purse while Marsha turned over their OPEN sign in the window. Their storefront had all glass windows, although they did not display their artwork there. Direct sunlight could damage their many paintings and sculptures. Instead, they had large canvases showing photos of the many works of art inside. Below the canvases, on antique white tables, were an array of ocean-themed items for decoration. Since the Promenade PV shopping area was a short distance from the beach, a beachy theme was what drew people inside.

Kristi met Marsha at the glass counter, where they displayed handmade gold and silver jewelry by local artisans. They didn't have a desk or cash register to ruin the look and flow of the shop. The interior was painted a soft aqua color with white trim and had a white plank-board ceiling with white beams. Marsha had wanted the place to exhibit a soothing environment as customers wandered the displays.

"Are you getting excited about the cruise?" Kristi asked. "I certainly am. A week in the Caribbean with my best friends and no kids," she said, laughing. "I don't know how I'll manage."

Marsha laughed along. "I can't wait. I'm so happy you and Jeffrey are coming along. Are your parents going to watch the children?"

"Yes," Kristi said. "They're coming to our house so the kids won't miss school. We haven't been on a vacation in years, so this will be nice."

Soon, customers came inside the gallery, and the two women became busy. They took turns getting lunch so one of them could keep an eye on the shop, and the day went by quickly.

"Are you sure Mari and Kevin will be fine running the gallery while we're away?" Marsha asked Kristi during a lull in the afternoon.

"They'll be fine. Don't worry. They run the gallery on the weekends and do a great job." Kristi shook her finger at her friend. "Don't you dare come up with an excuse not to go on the cruise."

Marsha chuckled. "I'm not. I'd close for a week if I had to.

There's no way I'm going to miss spending a week with Craig. He works so much; I feel like I hardly see him anymore."

Kristi left the shop at four to go home to her eight- and ten-year-old children, and Marsha closed at five and headed home. She made herself a light dinner and sat out on the veranda to enjoy the ocean view while she ate. She also made a list of all the things she needed to pack for their cruise, and the items she needed to buy. At nine o'clock, she checked her phone, surprised that Craig hadn't called her to say goodnight.

Once she was ready for bed, she checked her phone again. Craig was usually so scheduled he rarely missed calling her in the evening while he was away. He took trips to his offices often and was always good about staying in touch. Marsha thought about calling him, then thought he might have gone golfing that evening. She decided he'd probably eaten at the club with friends after golfing, and time slipped away from him.

Crawling into their king-sized bed, she lay back and smiled. Craig would be home the day after tomorrow, and maybe they'd take a long drive along the ocean on Saturday and enjoy the view. With that thought in mind, she fell asleep.

* * *

The next day, Marsha opened the gallery as usual and made a few phone calls to their favorite clients to tell them about the new items that had come into the shop. One client, in particular, had just built a five-thousand-square-foot home up the hill from her house with an incredible view of the ocean. She was working with a decorator and they were doing a modern motif throughout the home. Marsha thought Marco's new granite piece would be perfect for the woman.

Around noon, as Marsha went to the back room to get her purse and go buy lunch, her phone rang. She smiled, thinking it was probably Craig, but then saw it was a number she didn't recognize. Ignoring the call, Marsha walked back through the gallery as the phone rang again.

"Oh, these annoying telemarketers," Marsha said, stopping beside Kristi. Her friend nodded her understanding.

"Hello," Marsha said sharply, wanting to end the call immediately.

"Is this Mrs. Winslow?" an authoritative male voice asked on the other end of the line.

Marsha stood still for a moment, frowning. "Yes."

"Mrs. Winslow." The man's voice was suddenly gentler. "My name is Sergeant Terrance Riley of the Los Angeles Sheriff's Department in Malibu. I'm so sorry to inform you that your husband, Craig Winslow, has been in a car accident."

Marsha took a sudden breath and her hand flew to the heart necklace at her throat. "Is he okay?" she asked. Kristi moved closer to Marsha because of the distressed look on her face.

There was a pause that seemed to last an eternity.

"I'm sorry, ma'am. But your husband has died."

Marsha's eyes grew wide as she stared at Kristi.

"What's wrong?" Kristi asked, coming even closer.

"Craig's gone," Marsha whispered. Dizziness swept over her, and her knees went weak. Her beloved husband was dead.

Chapter Two

Marsha didn't know what she would have done if Jeffrey hadn't assisted her in all the morbid tasks of her husband's funeral. Those first two days after the devastating phone call, Marsha felt like she was in a haze of fog. She couldn't think straight or remember anything. Jeffrey immediately took charge. He went to Malibu to identify the body and then called the mortuary to pick up Craig's remains. Jeffrey drove Marsha to the funeral home and quietly assisted her in picking out a coffin and making all the arrangements for Craig's funeral. The Winslows had several family plots in a nice cemetery in Torrance, and it was decided to bury Craig near his parents and baby sister, who'd died at birth.

It was all so incredibly difficult.

"I just don't understand," Marsha said as she and Jeffrey got into his car to drive home after making the arrangements. "Why was Craig in Malibu? He said he was going to Monterey."

Jeffrey glanced over at his sister-in-law, looking unsure as to what to say. He was a handsome man, three years younger than Craig, with dark hair and kind brown eyes. He'd been in real estate since he was twenty and owned his own company.

Marsha had always respected Jeffrey's good business sense and his ability to find the right words in any situation. But right now, he seemed at a loss for words.

"Maybe Craig had said he was visiting the Malibu agency, and you thought he'd said Monterey," Jeffrey finally offered.

"Then why would he be there overnight when it's only an hour and a half away from home?" Marsha asked. She was desperate for answers. No one knew why the accident had occurred or why he'd been in Malibu. He'd simply driven off the road into a palm tree in someone's front yard. Why?

"Maybe he was in Monterey and came home a day early," Jeffrey said. He looked over at her, and she saw sadness in his eyes. Of course, Jeffrey was sad, too. He'd just lost his only brother and his last remaining family member.

"I'm so sorry," Marsha said, wiping tears from her eyes. All she did was cry now. She just couldn't stop. "You've lost your brother, and I'm grilling you for answers."

"Please don't be sorry. I wish I had the answers you're looking for," Jeffrey said, shaking his head. "I don't know if we'll ever know why the accident happened."

Jeffrey pulled into Marsha's driveway and stopped the car. "Are you sure you don't want to stay with Kristi and me for a few days?" His face held a pained expression.

"That's sweet of you both to invite me, but I'd rather be in my own home," Marsha said, stepping out of the car. She saw Jeffrey's worried expression and tried giving him a smile. "I'll be fine. Really. It'll be more comforting being around my memories of Craig."

Jeffrey nodded. "Call us if you need anything. Any time of the day or night."

"I will. Thank you for everything, Jeff. I couldn't have done all this without you." She gave him a slight wave and headed to the front door. Jeffrey waited with his headlights on until she was safely locked inside her house.

Locked inside with her memories of Craig.

Marsha walked through the dark house to the bedroom, trying not to see the photos on the hall table or the many items that she and Craig had purchased together through the years. Everything in the house had a memory attached. The painting by a local artist in the living room, the sculpture they'd purchased on their trip to Italy, and even the fine china that had been handed down from Craig's mother to Marsha. It all was connected to them as a couple, and while she cherished everything she owned, she'd give it all away just to spend one more day with her beloved husband.

Sighing, she switched on the nightstand light in the bedroom and changed into comfortable loungewear. She smiled as she changed, thinking about the first set of satin loungewear she'd purchased instead of wearing old sweats after a long day of work.

"So, we're moving up in the world, are we?" Craig had teased her. "No more sweats?"

"My satin loungewear is more befitting of this lovely home," she'd told him haughtily, and then they'd both laughed. She had come from a family that had to scrabble and save just to put clothes on their children's backs and food in their mouths. She was a sweatshirt kind of gal, but with Craig, she had blossomed into a silk and satin lady.

Walking into the kitchen, Marsha opened the freezer and stared at the contents. She didn't feel hungry, but she knew she should eat. She selected a package of Lean Cuisine, took it out of the box, and set it in the microwave. Marsha kept a few boxes of the frozen meals in the freezer for the nights when Craig was away. Now, she might have to stack the freezer with them for every night.

She shivered at the thought.

Three minutes later, she sat at the kitchen table with the light turned down low, eating her meal. She'd poured herself a glass of red wine to drink with her diet lasagna. Through the open window, she heard the sound of the ocean hitting the rocks below. It was a lonely sound—a sound she'd have to get used to for the rest of her life.

* * *

The funeral came quicker than Marsha was ready for, and as she sat in the front pew of the church, staring at her husband's gleaming oak coffin covered in flowers and greenery, she felt like she was living someone else's nightmare. She heard the minister's words and Jeffery's eulogy, but it sounded distant to her, like she was sitting at the end of a long tunnel. How could Craig be dead? It made no sense. And how could she be sitting here, listening to everyone speak about her husband in the past tense when he was surely going to walk through the door at any minute?

Marsha, Jeffrey, Kristi, and their two children stood at the church door after the service, thanking everyone who'd come. She smiled and nodded, not really listening to what each person said to her. With relief, the family slid into the limousine and rode silently to the cemetery. Again, nothing seemed real. The casket sitting above the open grave, the minister saying ashes to ashes, dust to dust. Marsha tried hard to concentrate but found herself looking out over the cemetery at all the graves and wondering why she was there. Even when Jeffrey placed his arm around her to indicate the graveside service was over and led her away, Marsha felt like this was all a bad dream.

Back at Kristi and Jeffrey's home, family, friends, and co-workers came to give their condolences and eat. Marsha wasn't hungry, and the last thing she wanted to do was make small talk with people. Didn't they know how deep her pain was? Why were they commenting on the beautiful weather or how lovely the service had been? It wasn't until Walter Carson, the office manager at Craig's Malibu office, came over to speak to Marsha that she finally was able to focus on a conversation.

"I'm so sorry, Marsha," Walter said, his wife, Jeanie, slowly nodding next to him. "Craig will certainly be missed by all of us."

"Thank you, Walter," Marsha said, staring at him. "Did you speak with Craig that day when he stopped by the office? Do you remember what time that was?"

Walter's forehead wrinkled as he stared back at Marsha. "I'm sorry," he said. "I didn't see Craig that day. Did he say he was stopping by the office to visit with us?"

Marsha frowned, confused by Walter's answer. Why wouldn't Craig stop by his office in Malibu? After all, Craig owned it.

"Thank you so much for coming, Walter. Craig would be pleased you're here," Jeffrey said, coming up beside Marsha.

Walter nodded and gave them both a smile before wandering off with his wife.

"Are you feeling okay?" Jeffrey asked Marsha, turning concerned eyes her way. "Maybe you'd like to sit down. Have you eaten anything?"

"I'm fine," Marsha said, sighing. "I'll just be glad when this day is over. It's too much."

"I agree," Jeffrey said quietly. "Why don't you grab a plate of food and sneak out to the terrace. Hopefully, people will start to leave soon."

Marsha wandered into the dining room, nodding and smiling at guests, and filled a plate with food that had been catered. It all smelled and looked delicious, but she had no appetite. She took her plate out to the terrace where none of the guests were and sat at the table, thankful for the silence. The view of the ocean from here was gorgeous, and she inhaled the ocean breeze, trying to clear her thoughts.

"Hey," a female voice said softly. "I brought you a glass of wine."

Marsha looked up and was relieved to see her dear friend, Kristi, was the one speaking.

"Thank you. I could use it about now," Marsha said.

"Do you want to be alone?" Kristi asked. Like Marsha, she wore a simple black dress and heels with a gold chain hanging around her neck. Marsha wore her heart pendant necklace and had touched it several times during the service.

"I want to be away from the crowd, but not from you," Marsha said. She patted the chair beside her. "Join me?"

Kristi sat, setting the glass of wine near Marsha. "It's been a terrible day."

Marsha sighed. "The worst! Thank you for not saying how lovely the weather is or what a nice service it was. It's the worst day of my life. Who cares how nice the weather is?"

"Amen!" Kristi said, sitting back in her chair. "I wish I could say something, anything, that would make you feel better, but I can't think of one thing. I try putting myself in your shoes, and I realize just how devastated I'd be if I were in your place. I'm so sorry, Marsha. You know how much I love you and loved Craig. It's all so terrible."

Tears filled Marsha's eyes for the first time that day. The sterile service and the minister's words had not moved her to tears, but Kristi's had. Because Kristi knew Craig, and how much Marsha had loved him. "Thank you for that. I've had to be strong for everyone coming to the service and reception today, but now it's just us, and I can finally feel something."

Kristi reached over and hugged her friend, and Marsha clung to her.

"What will I do without him?" Marsha asked, sobbing. "He was my entire life."

"I don't know," Kristi said, also crying. "But I'm here for you, and we'll take it one step at a time."

Marsha nodded. Yes. That was all she could do. Take things one day, one step at a time. But for now, she let the tears flow.

* * *

Marsha got through the next couple of days as best she could. She had busy work to do, filling out forms, changing bank accounts, and taking Craig's name off of the bills. On Monday, she had an appointment with Craig's long-time attorney to go over the will and finances. Even though Marsha had once taken care of the business's finances, since it had grown, they'd handed that over to an accountant. She knew they were well off but wasn't completely sure of every aspect of their finances.

Jeffrey offered to drive her to the lawyer's office, but Marsha declined. She knew she had to stop leaning on Kristi and Jeffrey and start taking care of things herself. Dressed in a charcoal suit and white blouse, she drove into Torrance to Richard Everson's office. Richard had once been a partner in a booming law firm but had semi-retired and only kept his most valued clients. His office was a cute little Spanish style building among a row of other professional offices. Letitia, his assistant, greeted Marsha at the front desk and led her to Richard's office.

Richard stood and smiled when Marsha entered the office. He was a short, stout, serious-looking man, but Marsha knew he had a kind heart. He shook her hand warmly before offering her a chair in front of his cluttered walnut desk.

"Would you like anything to drink?" Letitia asked Marsha.

"No, thank you. I'm fine," she responded, and the assistant left the room.

"I am so sorry for your loss," Richard said as he sat down again. "I know I already said that at the funeral, but Craig will be deeply missed by all. I've worked on his legal affairs for decades, but I've also known you both as friends."

"Thank you, Richard," Marsha said, forcing back the tears that burned in her eyes. "It still doesn't feel real. I think I'm still in shock."

"I completely understand. Unfortunately, this is a part of my job that I must do regularly, and it's always hard when someone passes on." Richard shuffled papers on his desk and lifted a large folder. "We have a lot to go through. I hope you're up to it."

Marsha nodded. Richard put on his half-moon reading glasses and opened the folder. "Your accountant sent over the latest figures for me to go over with you. Since I was named the executor of the will, I was privy to that information."

"I understand," Marsha said distractedly. She knew where she and Craig stood on their finances. Their house was paid off, and they owned the three insurance businesses along with her art gallery. She just needed to decide what to do with everything now that Craig was gone.

"Well, I'm afraid things haven't been going as well with Craig's business as it once had," Richard said. "Although selling the offices in Monterey and Malibu helped him keep the Torrance office opened."

Marsha sat up straighter, wondering if she'd heard right. "Selling the offices? Craig sold his offices in Monterey and Malibu?"

Richard looked up at her. "Yes. He sold the Monterey office three years ago and the Malibu one two years ago. The employees of both offices pooled together to buy each business. I assumed you knew."

Marsha frowned as her conversation with Walter from the Malibu office came back to her. No wonder he'd looked at her strangely when she'd asked if Craig had visited the office. Why would he if he no longer owned it?

"So, let me get this straight. We only own the Torrance insurance office?" Marsha asked.

"Yes. And the art gallery as well, although you rent that building. And, as you already know, that venture has been running in the red since it opened."

Once again, Marsha couldn't comprehend what Richard was saying. "In the red? Our gallery does quite well with sales. Craig never said it was losing money."

Richard stared over his glasses at Marsha. "I'm sorry. But the paperwork here shows your expenses far exceed your income." He handed the monthly reports to her to look over. "Didn't Craig share this information with you?"

Marsha sighed as she glanced at the reports. No, Craig hadn't said a thing. And she hadn't asked, either. She had happily handed over her paperwork to the accountant to take care of, and had believed her gallery was doing well.

"No, he didn't. Craig knew how much I loved owning the gallery. He must have thought we could use it as a write-off."

Richard nodded. "I'm sorry. The good news is you own the Palos Verdes home and the one insurance business. Maybe you could sell that."

Marsha nodded. She had no desire to run the office by herself. But how would she earn an income without it if the gallery wasn't earning money? "I'll have to think about it."

"Oh, and there is the Malibu home, although there is a mortgage on it." Richard looked up at her. "That would be the perfect property to sell. I'm sure it's gained quite a bit of equity over the decade that you've owned it."

Marsha felt like she'd been hit by a truck. The Malibu house? "What Malibu house?" she finally asked.

Richard's brows shot up. "Oh, I'm sorry. I thought you knew about that, too. Craig bought the house up on the hillside overlooking the ocean about eight years ago. He said it was a great fixer-upper that would gain equity quickly. I had no idea you didn't know about it."

"It seems there's a lot I don't know about," Marsha said tightly.

"Well, yes. I'm sorry. But your name is also on the title, so you'll be able to sell it easily if you decide to do so. Here." He handed her a folder with the title and a spare set of keys. "Craig wanted me to have a set of keys in case something happened to him."

Marsha stared at the manila folder in her hands. This was unbelievable. Craig owned a house that he'd never told her about. "Are there any more surprises?" Marsha asked.

Richard glanced over the paperwork. "That seems to cover it. Everything was left to you in the will, with the exception of a few personal items he wanted his brother, Jeffery, to have. Let me see." Richard rifled through the sheets. "Ah, yes. The watch that had belonged to their father as well as their grandfather's pocket watch. He wanted those given to his brother."

"Of course," Marsha said.

Richard took off his glasses and looked at Marsha kindly. "I'm so sorry all this has come as a surprise to you. Craig loved you very much. It makes no sense that he kept secrets."

"But he did," Marsha said sharply, then regretted it. After all, Craig may have had good reasons for not telling her about selling the businesses or buying the house. "I guess we'll never know now."

"Well, the Malibu house just might be a blessing. With rising property values in those neighborhoods and all the homes lost from the Palisades fires this year, you might make a nice profit selling that house. Or renting it if you choose to keep it. I'd suggest going to see it as soon as possible to decide the best course of action," Richard said.

"I will," Marsha told him, standing up.

Richard stood, too, and handed Marsha the thick folder. "The mortuary sent over several copies of Craig's death certificate for you. If you need any legal advice at all, please call me."

"I will," Marsha said, forcing a smile. They said goodbye, and she walked outside into the sunshine and slipped into her car. Marsha sat there for a long while, staring at the folder in the seat beside her. Why had Craig kept so many secrets from her? Why not tell her he wanted to sell the businesses or that he wanted to buy a second house as an investment? She'd always thought their relationship was open and honest. Now, she was confused.

What else was she going to find out now that her husband was gone?

Chapter Three

Not quite sure where to go or what to do with herself, Marsha automatically drove to her art gallery. She left the folder in her car and walked into the shop. It was empty, except for Kristi standing behind the jewelry case, cleaning the glass.

"Marsha. I didn't expect to see you here today," Kristi said, coming around the counter to stand beside her friend. "Didn't you have a meeting with your lawyer today?"

Marsha nodded. "I did. And I wasn't sure what to do with myself afterward." She walked toward the back room, and Kristi followed.

"Is everything okay? You look a bit stunned," Kristi asked.

Marsha set her purse on top of the desk and turned to face her friend. Could she tell Kristi how betrayed she felt over having been left out of Craig's business decisions? Since she hadn't had time to process the information herself, Marsha didn't feel she could share it quite yet.

"I just have a lot to think about," Marsha finally said, then locked her purse in the bottom drawer. Kristi nodded as if she understood.

"If Jeffrey or I can help you in any way, please don't hesitate to ask," Kristi said. "We're always here for you."

Marsha smiled. "Thank you. I know you are. I think I need time to process what I need to do."

The bell on the front door jingled softly, announcing a customer. Kristi headed out to the gallery. Marsha stayed in the office for a moment, thinking about everything Richard had told her. She'd have to tell Kristi at some point that their shop wasn't profitable, and they'd need to come up with a solution to change that. If they couldn't make money at the gallery, they'd have to close it. That thought hurt Marsha's heart. She'd already lost the most important person in her life. She couldn't bear to lose her beloved gallery as well.

Standing up straight and squaring her shoulders, she walked out onto the gallery floor. *First things first,* she thought. She'd look over the receipts from the past few months and see how she could make the gallery profitable. Then, when she was ready, she'd drive to Malibu and see the house that Craig had purchased. It would take time and all the energy she had to take care of her finances so she would be able to support herself.

The thought of all she had to do weighed heavily on her.

Marsha spent two days going over receipts and expenses for the gallery, trying to figure out what they could do to make more money. Even though Kristi was a partner in the business, she didn't tell her why she was doing this. She thought it would be better to have solutions before telling her the problem. Besides, immersing herself in the finances helped take her mind off of losing Craig.

Evenings at home alone with her memories were the hardest part of each day. Marsha would make herself dinner and sit at the dining table alone, watching the ocean view. It was soothing but not enough to keep her from thinking how silent her nights were now. And lonely.

Her thoughts wandered, too. She wondered why Craig hadn't discussed his businesses with her or the sale of the two insurance offices. They'd always worked as a team, so why hide it from her? And the house in Malibu. To buy a house eight years ago and never mention it was so out of character for Craig. By the time he'd bought it, they'd already been married for eleven years and had purchased their own home. Why would he need another home? Her mind went to several different scenarios—all of which she didn't like. She hoped it was just an investment opportunity for him and nothing more.

On Friday, she finally forced herself to stop by the Torrance office to check on it. When she walked inside the building, Carla, the receptionist who'd worked there for ten years, greeted her with a hug.

"I'm so sorry about Craig," Carla said softly. "I know we talked at the funeral, but it still doesn't feel real. I'm sure you're still trying to process it."

"I am," Marsha said. She smiled at Carla, who she'd person-ally hired when she stopped working at the insurance office. "But I thought I should check in and see how things were going here."

Carla wrapped her arm around Marsha's waist and led her to Justin's office. He was a sales agent and the office manager who Craig had hired years before.

"Someone here to see you," Carla said cheerfully to Justin.

He quickly stood from behind his desk. "Marsha. It's so great to see you." He walked around his desk and hugged her.

"I just wanted to check in," Marsha said, looking up at Justin. He was tall with dark hair and eyes. Craig had made him the office manager a few years ago because Craig was always traveling between his offices. Which seemed odd now since Marsha knew Craig had sold the other two offices. Once again, the question came to her. *Where had Craig been going on his trips to the other offices?*

"Can I get you something?" Carla asked, interrupting Marsha's thoughts. "Coffee? Water?"

"No, thank you, dear. I'm fine," Marsha said.

Carla smiled and nodded, then exited the room.

"Please, sit down," Justin said. "Since Craig's passing, I've been going over the office's books because I knew you'd want to see them."

Marsha sat, noticing the stack of papers spread all over Justin's desk. "Looks like you've had a lot to go through," she said, chuckling.

He smiled. "Yes. But I've been trying to get everything in order for quite a while. Before Craig died, he'd talked about selling the office to the employees as he'd done with his other two offices."

Marsha's brows shot up. "Oh. I had no idea."

"I'm sorry. I thought he would have mentioned it to you," Justin said. "Craig asked me to go over the finances, and together, we'd come up with a price to sell the business. We were hoping to have it completed by the end of the year."

Marsha was dumbstruck. She had come in to talk about the income the office was bringing in so she'd know what she had to work with. But now she was hit with selling the office.

"Maybe I should have my lawyer speak with you about this," she said. "He'd know better how much Craig sold the other two offices for and what this one might be worth."

Justin nodded. "The entire team would really like to make

the deal work."

"I understand," Marsha said. "I'm just not sure I can sell it right now. I'll be in need of a regular income as well."

"Oh." Justin looked confused. "I thought Craig and you were financially set. Craig talked about retiring."

"To be honest, Justin, that's news to me. But as I said, once you have a proposal, I'll have my lawyer look at it. If I can afford to sell, then I might want to. I've just been hit with a lot of changes all of a sudden."

"Yes. Of course, you have. And I'm sorry to add this to your plate. I had no idea Craig hadn't shared this with you."

Marsha nodded and stood. "Thanks for telling me. Let me know when you're ready to make an offer. I'd also like to look over the finances to see what the office earns in a year. Can you send me the financial statements when you get a chance?"

"I can email them to you later this afternoon," he said, smiling. "I almost have everything in order."

"Wonderful. I'll talk to you soon," Marsha said. She walked out of his office and nearly bumped into Glenda, the other agent who worked there. "Oh, Glenda. I'm so sorry. My mind was elsewhere."

"That's understandable," Glenda said, smiling at her. Glenda was a tall blonde in her mid-forties. She'd worked for Craig for years. "How are you?"

Marsha sighed. "Okay, considering. I've been hit with a lot over the past few days. I'm just trying to figure out what needs to be done."

Glenda nodded. "Craig will be missed. We all adored him. He was the perfect boss."

"Thank you, dear. I certainly can attest to that." Marsha said goodbye and waved to Carla on the way out. Once she was in her car, she just stared straight ahead of her. So much had been going on in Craig's life and she hadn't had a clue about any of it. It baffled her that he'd kept so many secrets from her.

Marsha drove to the art gallery and got there in time to let Kristi leave at her usual time. "Sorry you've been stuck here all week," Marsha told her. "There's just been a lot going on."

Kristi smiled. "I wasn't stuck here. But it will be nice to get home early tonight. And Mari and Kevin will be running the gallery this weekend, so we both can have time off. I'm sure you could use a breather from everything at this point."

Marsha nodded. "There was so much I had no idea Craig was involved in. I always thought he confided everything in me, but I'm learning differently. I have no idea what to think."

Kristi tilted her head and stared at Marsha. "Really? That surprises me. You and Craig were the closest couple I've ever known. Do you want to talk about it?"

Marsha waved her hand in the air. "I don't want to take up your time tonight. Go along home, we can talk on Monday. Enjoy your kids and your weekend."

Kristi frowned. "Are you sure there isn't anything I can do to help?"

"You just being here and willing to work longer hours while I sort things out is help enough," Marsha said. She hugged her friend. "I promise I'll tell you everything once I figure it all out."

That evening, Marsha picked up a pita sandwich and salad on her way home and sat alone, once again, at the dining room table, eating her dinner. It was cloudy out, and she could see rain coming toward the house across the ocean. She felt exactly like the weather looked—cloudy, dismal, and depressed. What had Craig been thinking, selling off his businesses and buying a second house? If she hadn't known better, she would have thought he was planning on leaving her. But he'd bought the house years ago and sold the businesses a while back. And he'd been excited about their upcoming cruise for their anniversary. So, why keep secrets?

"Oh, Craig," Marsha said, touching the heart pendant hanging around her neck. "What have you been hiding from me?"

With a sigh, Marsha put her dishes in the dishwasher and went to change into night clothes. It was going to be another long, lonely night.

* * *

The next day, the sky had cleared, and it was another perfect Southern California day. Marsha dressed in jeans, a white blouse, and flats, all the while forcing herself not to think about what she was doing that day. She put on a light touch of make-up and did her hair. Then, having no other reason to procrastinate, she took the folder the lawyer had given her and headed out to her car.

It was time to see the house in Malibu.

Marsha looked inside the folder and typed the house address into her map app on her phone. She also took the one key taped to the paperwork and slipped it into her pocket.

The drive to Malibu took her an hour and a half. The landscape had changed greatly since the Palisades and Malibu fires, and it broke her heart to see it this way. She could tell there had been a lot of clearing up where houses used to stand and some new construction. Marsha was happy people were rebuilding in the area.

She took a right onto a road directly across from Big Rock Beach and wound her way through a neighborhood that looked to have been built in the 1960s and 70s. She turned left into another neighborhood and soon stopped in front of a house on the right side of the road with the house number on it that she was looking for.

Marsha sat in her car for a moment and studied the home. It was a long, ranch-style design that looked to have been updated recently. There were large windows in the front, possibly the living room, and the steps up to the house and the driveway were done with flagstone pavers. The yard was large, with beautiful, lush landscaping.

And it didn't look like anyone was moving around inside.

Stepping out of her car, Marsha walked up the paver steps to the front door. She turned a moment and gazed at the lovely view of the ocean down below. The homes on the opposite side of the street were at a lower level, allowing a beautiful view. Maybe not as dramatic as her Palos Verdes home, but still gorgeous.

Marsha pulled the key from her pocket and unlocked the door. As soon as she heard the lock click and give way, she knew she was at the right place. She stepped inside a bright, cozy living room with cream sofas and a Spanish-style fireplace lined with red brick. Walking farther into the house, she saw the dining room and kitchen. Both rooms were clean but looked like they'd recently been used.

"Did you stay here sometimes?" Marsha asked Craig aloud, knowing he couldn't answer her. She walked to the dining room window and peered outside. The backyard was large, with a beautiful patio, a grassy area, and a tiered garden. From here, you couldn't see the house that was surely behind it because of the large bushes.

It was a beautiful house, from what Marsha could tell. Definitely a place where Craig would feel at home. Marsha turned and noticed a row of photos on a sideboard in the dining room. She panicked. Was the house being rented out and she was trespassing? Still, the photos drew her in. In one, a woman with long dark hair and an olive complexion smiled up at the camera from a chair in the backyard, hugging a young boy, possibly six years old. In another, the woman and boy were standing in the water at the beach, smiling and splashing around. The boy looked younger in the photo, around three. She looked down the line of photos, and in each, something about the boy's face seemed familiar. His smile and the shape of his dark brown eyes reminded her of someone. When she reached the last photo, her heart beat faster. Standing on the beach with the sun setting in the background was the pretty woman, the little boy, and a man with his arms around them. She knew now why she recognized the little boy's eyes. They were exactly like his father's. Craig.

Marsha took in a breath and backed up into a chair, nearly tipping it over. At that exact moment, she heard someone coming in through the front door.

A woman was laughing as she told someone not to run into the house with his shoes on. "You'll get sand all over the house," the woman said.

Marsha stepped into the hallway between the dining room and living room and stared directly at the woman and her son. The woman was startled and reached for her boy but just stood there, staring back.

As Marsha stared at the woman, her eyes went to the heart pendant necklace hanging around the woman's neck. Marsha lifted her hand up to touch her own pendant. Reality hit her like a brick. Marsha rushed past the woman and the boy, out the door, and to her car.

Her heart was shattered.

Chapter Four

Without even thinking, Marsha drove out of the neighborhood as fast as she could and down to Highway One. Her mind was racing, and she had trouble focusing on where she was going. Who was the woman living in Craig's house? And why did the boy look just like him? Her mind had trouble accepting that he had another woman in his life—another family. That wasn't like Craig. He was always an attentive, loving husband. But the proof was in the photo of the small family on the sideboard.

Craig had been cheating on her for years.

Over an hour later, she realized she didn't want to go home. She spun the car around and headed north again toward Redondo Beach. Up ahead, she saw Craig's face looming above the highway, smiling down at her. The billboard that once brought her joy when passing it now seemed to mock her. She rushed past it and before she knew it, she was parked in front of Jeffrey and Kristi's house.

She sat in the car a moment, wondering if what she'd seen was real. Had she imagined the photo of Craig with the woman and boy? Had she imagined the resemblance between the boy and Craig? No, it was not her imagination. The house Craig had never told her about, the woman and the little boy who lived there, and the same necklace as Marsha's around the woman's neck were not her imagination. Craig had a relationship with another woman and had a child with her.

Tears filled Marsha's eyes. Why hadn't Craig told her about the woman and his son? Why would he stay with her all these years while maintaining a house for them? It was bad enough that Craig had another woman in his life, but to also have a child with that woman was unforgivable. A child. The only thing that Marsha was never able to give him.

Swiping the tears from her eyes, Marsha grabbed the folder with the house's information in it and walked up to the door. Kristi opened it before she knocked.

"Marsha. I saw you sitting in your car. Is everything okay?"

"No," Marsha said, walking past Kristi into the house. "Everything is not okay. Is Jeffrey here?"

"He's out back with the kids. I'll get him," Kristi said, staring at her friend strangely.

"Thank you." Marsha opened the folder and stared at the paperwork. There, at the bottom, was what she'd suspected would be there. Jeffrey's signature as the selling agent for the house. Jeffrey had found and sold the Malibu house to his brother.

"Hey, Marsha. What's going on?" Jeffrey said, his tone friendly. But when he saw the folder in her hands, his expression changed.

"You knew all along, didn't you?" Marsha said, shaking the folder at him. "You sold Craig the house."

Jeffrey stood there, silent.

"Knew what?" Kristi asked, staring at her husband, then

Marsha. "What's going on?"

Marsha glanced out the window to make sure the kids were still outside. "Jeffrey knew that Craig had bought a house for his girlfriend. And his son."

Kristi's eyes widened. "What?"

Jeffrey took a deep breath. "I knew, yes," he said softly. "I'm sorry, Marsha. I didn't approve of what he'd done, but he was my brother. So, I helped him."

Hot tears slid down Marsha's face. "How could you? I thought you were my friend. I thought I could trust my husband and you. But you both betrayed me." She sat heavily in a chair and dropped her face in her hands. "Nothing about my life was true. It was all a lie. A lie I believed."

Jeffrey dropped to his knees in front of her. "No, Marsha. That's not true. Craig loved you more than anything in the world. But he made a mistake, and being the person that he was, he couldn't just walk away from that mistake. But he loved you. Believe me."

Marsha lifted her tear-stained face and stared hard at him. "I don't believe you. I can't believe anything you say to me anymore." She stood, grabbed the folder, and headed for the door.

"Marsha! Please!" Kristi called, running after her. "You have to know I didn't know any of this. I would never have kept this a secret from you."

Marsha turned and looked at her friend. Yes, she knew Kristi had been in the dark, too. Kristi would have told her if she'd known. "I believe you. But it doesn't change anything. My life with Craig was a lie. A terrible, horrible lie." She walked out the door and to her car, then drove away.

Driving again on Highway One toward home, Marsha's

rage burned inside of her. Not only had her husband cheated on her, but he'd kept his girlfriend in a nice house and had a child with her. That was what hurt the most. Craig and she had tried for so long to have children, but it never happened. Had he had an affair just so he could have a child? Her heart was torn into pieces, and she was so enraged she could barely see straight.

The sun was setting into the ocean as she turned a curve and saw that stupid billboard again, smiling down at her. Fueled by her anger, Marsha pulled onto a gravel turnout, stopped her car, and stepped outside.

"How dare you smile down at me, you lousy bastard!" she screamed up at Craig's sign. "You cheated on me! You turned our marriage into a sham!"

Cars drove by as Marsha stood there on the side of the road, raging at the sign. She remembered her once treasured heart necklace and pulled it from her neck, breaking the chain. "You gave her this exact same necklace! How could you?" She screamed. "You said you'd given me your heart for eternity. Did you tell her that too?" Marsha was so angry she threw down the necklace and then bent to pick up stones from the gravel. She threw them at the billboard. "I hate you!" she screamed, dropping down to pick up more stones and throwing them. "You're a liar and a cheater! I hate you!"

Marsha was so furious that she hadn't heard a car pull up behind her. As she threw more stones at her husband's picture, two strong hands gently touched her arms.

"Ma'am? Are you okay? Can I help you?" a male voice asked from behind her.

She stopped immediately and went limp. The man grasped her arms tighter so she wouldn't fall onto the ground.

"Ma'am? Are you okay? Ma'am?"

Marsha took a deep breath and stood up straight again, turning to see who was speaking to her. A tall man in a Los Angeles Police Department uniform looked down at her with concern etched on his face. Behind him, a young man in uniform stood also, looking confused.

"I'm so sorry," Marsha said, fresh tears streaming down her face. "I don't know what came over me."

The officer studied her a moment, and then he looked up at the billboard and back at Marsha. "Oh. I'm sorry," he said, sounding sincere. "Craig Winslow passed away recently. Was he your husband?"

Marsha felt shattered. The tears fell faster as she nodded her answer.

"I'm so sorry, Ma'am." The officer glanced around and then seemed to come to a decision. "Do you live near here?"

"Yes," she said in barely a whisper. "A few miles up the road."

The officer turned and opened the passenger door of Marsha's car. "Please sit down, Ma'am."

She sat in the car, still crying.

"I'm going to drive Mrs. Winslow home, Curt," the officer called out to the other police officer. "Follow me there."

Curt nodded and got back into the squad car.

Marsha watched as the officer carefully closed her door, then bent to pick something up. He ran around to the driver's side and sat behind the wheel.

"I found this on the ground," he told her, opening his hand to reveal Marsha's heart necklace.

"Thank you," she said, letting him drop it into her open hand. Her anger from moments ago had abated, and now she only felt numb.

The officer pulled down the visor, found the registration, and copied the home address into his phone. "I'll have you home in a few minutes," he said kindly. "I'm Officer Mike Becker, by the way. Just so it doesn't feel weird having a stranger drive you home."

Marsha nodded. She knew if she uttered a word, she'd start crying again. Her nerves were that raw.

Officer Becker had her home in minutes and pulled her car into her driveway. He stepped out of the car and ran around to her side, opening the door for her. By now, it was completely dark out except for the motion lights that had come on over her garage and at the door. Without a word, he escorted her to the front door.

"Thank you, Officer," Marsha said. "I was a mess back there. It was kind of you to help me."

He smiled. "We all have bad days. I'm sorry again about your husband."

"Thank you," she said.

With a nod, Officer Becker walked to the squad car where his partner was waiting for him.

Marsha went inside the dark house and made her way to the bedroom without turning on the lights. She dropped the broken necklace on her nightstand and fell onto her bed.

The tears flowed easily.

* * *

The next morning, Marsha awoke feeling like she'd been on a bender. Her head ached, and her eyes were sore and puffy. She felt sick to her stomach as well, but she attributed that to not having eaten since the day before. Sometime during the night, she'd awoken enough to change into pajamas and crawl under the covers. Now, she was desperate for some Tylenol and food.

She stumbled into the kitchen to check the contents of her refrigerator and was surprised to see the wall clock read it was past eleven a.m. Marsha never slept that late, but this morning was an exception. After all, how many times in a woman's life does she learn that her deceased husband had another family? And then be picked up by the police for attacking a billboard. It would be funny if it didn't feel so tragic.

There was a knock on her front door, and for a second, Marsha thought about not answering. Maybe it was the officer stopping by to check on her or Jeffrey coming to apologize. The way she felt, she didn't want to see either one of them. Despite that, Marsha walked to the door and instead saw Kristi standing there with a bakery box in hand and two coffees.

"I hope I'm not bothering you," Kristi said once Marsha opened the door. "But I couldn't just let things stand as they were yesterday. You're my best friend!"

"It's okay," Marsha said calmly. "Just ignore how I look. I had a rough night."

Kristi walked in and set the box and coffee cups on the kitchen counter. Marsha watched her as her mind went back to the day when she and Craig had hand-picked the large granite stone that would become their countertops. There were so many memories in every corner of the house.

"What happened last night?" Kristi asked, handing Marsha one of the coffee cups and opening the box. "You didn't get in an accident, did you?"

Marsha shook her head. She was starving, so she lifted one of the blueberry muffins from the box and walked over to the dining room table to sit down.

Kristi took one also and followed her, sitting in the chair across from her friend. "I'm so sorry about everything. I knew nothing about the Malibu house or that Craig was involved with another woman. You must believe me."

Marsha took a bite of the muffin. It was still warm and delicious. Sighing, she smiled wanly at her friend. "I do believe you. I'm sure it wasn't something that Jeffrey would have wanted to share with you."

"Well, I'm definitely angry with him," Kristi said. Her blue eyes shone brightly. "I made him tell me everything he knew. Jeffrey said that he had helped Craig find a house, but had thought it was for investment purposes. He said the house was a fixer-upper, and Craig got it for a good price, then had it remodeled. It wasn't until after he'd purchased it that he told Jeff to not mention the house to you, and that's when Jeffrey drew the truth out of him."

Marsha continued to eat her muffin in between sips of coffee. She was trying to take in everything Kristi said, but her mind wasn't working that quickly. But she knew that Jeffrey was a good person and wouldn't have condoned what Craig had done to her.

"They were brothers," Marsha finally said. "Jeffrey had no choice but to keep it a secret."

Kristi shook her head. "That's what Jeffrey said, but I still think he should have told you. You had a right to know."

Did she? Marsha thought. If she'd known eight years ago that Craig had a woman on the side and a son as well and had bought them a house, in which he obviously spent time with them all these years, how different would her life be?

Kristi placed a hand on Marsha's arm. "I asked Jeffrey to

tell me the whole story. Do you want to hear it?" she asked softly.

Marsha nodded. She knew it would tear her apart, but she needed to know how it happened.

Kristi took a breath. "He met the woman when she started working for him as a receptionist in the Malibu office. She was there about a year before they, well, had a one-night stand, and then three months later, she told him she was pregnant."

Marsha closed her eyes. Pregnant. How many times in the first ten years of their marriage had she tried to get pregnant? And Craig had always told her that it was fine. He had her, and if they didn't have children, he was more than happy as long as he had her.

"Jeff said Craig swore he'd never cheated on you before and hadn't ever wanted to. But something happened, and he was drawn to this woman. Anyway, once he heard she was pregnant, he found her a nicer apartment than she was living in and promised to be there for the child. After the child was born, and he knew for sure it was his, he bought the house and moved them in."

"And he fell in love with her," Marsha said, standing up and walking to the window.

Kristi stood, too, and walked over to her. "I guess he spent a lot of time with her and his son, but there's no proof he loved her. He loved you. He couldn't wait to celebrate your anniversary. Jeff said that Craig found himself in a sticky situation and his kind heart wouldn't let him walk away from her and his son. And there was no way he wanted to leave you."

"Yeah, so he had the best of both worlds," Marsha said bitterly. "Poor guy."

"I'm sorry, Marsha. I really am. I can't even imagine how

you feel right now. But I still believe Craig loved you more than anyone else," Kristi said.

Marsha turned and looked at her friend. "That's a nice sentiment, but we'll never know if it's true. That woman was wearing the same necklace Craig gave me for our fifteenth wedding anniversary. The exact same necklace! So, I guess he gave his heart to her and to me."

"Oh, I had no idea," Kristi said, looking shocked. "I thought we all knew Craig better than that, but I guess we didn't know him at all."

"No, we didn't. Think about how it makes you feel and multiply it by a thousand, and then you'll understand how I feel." Marsha shook her head. "He lied to me about so many things. And now I have to clean up his mess."

"I'm sorry," Kristi said. She stepped up to Marsha and hugged her. "I wish there was something I could do to help you."

"Thanks, honey," Marsha said, hugging her back. She pulled away. "And thank you for telling me all this. The good news is Craig left everything to me. The bad news is he left me deep in debt. Somehow, I'll have to dig my way out of it."

Kristi stared at her. "Would you sell the house in Malibu?"

"I can't keep it. It has a mortgage, and the taxes are high. And I'm certainly not going to rent it to Craig's mistress," Marsha spat. "I have to start getting things in order. And it's more than I want to do at this moment."

"I'll help you in any way I can," Kristi said. "Just name it."

"Thanks. We'll have enough to worry about with the art gallery. Apparently, it's hemorrhaging money," Marsha said. When she saw Kristi's shocked reaction, she raised her hands to silence any questions she might have. "We'll worry about that soon enough, though. Right now, I just need to figure out my finances and try to keep my head above water."

"You should take some time for yourself," Kristi suggested. "I can take care of the gallery. No one expects you to rush into anything so soon after Craig's death."

Marsha laughed. "I can't afford time off, thanks to my beloved husband. No, I'll come into work tomorrow as usual and try to find ways to keep the gallery open. There's so much for us to do."

Kristi left after that, leaving Marsha alone once again in her house full of memories. Tomorrow, she'd take on the world. But today, she was going to give in to her anger and sadness and try to let it all go. If only it was that easy.

Chapter Five

Marsha awoke early the next morning, showered, and put on her make-up as usual, making sure to use a lot of concealer for her puffy eyes. She'd spent the previous day walking on the beach and feeling heartbroken. Then, in a fit of rage, she found a big box in the garage and packed up all of Craig's expensive suits, shirts, and ties—everything. Maybe if she didn't have to look at his things, she'd feel better. Unfortunately, it didn't work.

Sighing as she finished styling her hair, Marsha looked at the clock. She had one business call to attend to before she drove to the gallery.

Standing in front of her living room window to soothe herself with the ocean view, Marsha took a deep breath and dialed her lawyer.

"Marsha." Richard sounded happy to hear from her. "I'm so glad you called. What can I do for you?"

"Hi, Richard. I've been thinking a lot about my options for taking care of my finances, and I'd like to sell the house in Malibu. But before I can do that, I'll need someone to send a notice to the people living in it that they have until the end of the month to vacate the premises."

"Oh." Richard sounded confused. "I wasn't aware that Craig was renting it."

Marsha heard papers being shuffled around through the line before Richard continued speaking. "There's no mention of rental income in Craig's income spreadsheet."

"Yes, well, I'm pretty sure this person hasn't been paying rent. However, Craig was aware of her. So, I'd like you to send her an official letter stating that she must be out by the end of September. If you need her name and address, you can call Jeffrey. He knows all about her," Marsha said, her last few words terse.

"Ah, I see," Richard said. From the tone of his voice, Marsha could tell he'd known nothing of the other woman in Craig's life. "I'll do that right away. It's a sound business move to sell that house with how high property values are today."

"Thank you, Richard. I'll let you know once we put the house on the market and sell it," Marsha told him.

After she hung up, she was surprised she didn't feel better about her decision. She thought sending Craig's secret family packing from the house would give her some level of satisfaction, but instead, she questioned whether she was doing the right thing.

"That woman is not my problem," she said aloud to the empty house. "And neither is the boy." A part of her wished Craig could hear her right now. Another part of her was glad he couldn't.

Grabbing her purse and a light jacket, Marsha walked through the connecting door to the garage and to her car. She tried not to look at the large box of Craig's clothing in the corner. Pulling out, she drove to the gallery.

Marsha arrived half an hour early, but Kristi was already there.

"Hi," Kristi said from behind the jewelry counter. She had paperwork from the weekend in front of her. "I was just writing up the bank deposit from the weekend."

"Did Mari and Kevin have a profitable weekend?" Marsha asked hopefully.

"They sold a few items. The Malibu seascape sold, and so did the one of the Pacific Palisade's cliffs."

Marsha nodded. "Jermaine and Lisa will be happy to get their commission on those. I'll be right back." She walked into the back room to put away her purse and jacket. Selling two paintings was good, but not good enough. They had to try to sell the larger pieces to survive.

Carrying a folder of client's names out with her, Marsha returned to the front of the store. "Maybe we need to be a little more aggressive and start calling our regular clients about items that come into the gallery," she said to Kristi. "Like the sculpture by Marco. Instead of waiting for someone to see it and buy it, let's call Anita and urge her to come see it. She's still decorating her home, and it would be perfect for her."

Kristi frowned. "I'm sure it's a good idea, but you used to say you didn't want to push people into buying items. Won't we appear desperate?"

Marsha sighed. "Frankly, we are desperate. The sooner we sell this sculpture, the sooner Marco will give us another to sell. That's good money and good business sense. We have a list of regular clients we should be constantly contacting to let them know about new items. It's not pushy—it's business."

"Will you please tell me what's going on?" Kristi asked. "After all, I'm part owner of this gallery too. We should make these decisions together."

"You're right," Marsha said. "I've just been so worried that we might lose this place that I've shut you out. Our business has been running in the red since we opened it. Craig has been making up our losses by adding money to the business without my knowledge. Since I let the accountant take care of everything, all I knew was the income that came in and the commissions to the artists going out. He never told me that we ran this at a loss."

"He should have told us," Kristi said, sounding upset. "If we'd known, we could have tried to fix the problem. Here all along I thought we could afford to pay ourselves for working here each month. Yet the whole time, Craig was just keeping us afloat. I thought we had a successful business."

"Welcome to my world," Marsha said sadly. "I thought we were successful too. I had no idea. And I didn't ask because I liked thinking we were successful. I guess I should have asked a lot of questions that I didn't."

"Oh, I'm sorry, Marsha," Kristi said, suddenly remorseful. "I shouldn't be angry with Craig. After all, he's gone and can't defend himself. And you've been through so much."

"Yes, I have," Marsha said. "But I can't deny that Craig put me in this position. And now I have to dig us out."

"We have to dig us out together," Kristi said sternly. "Don't put this all on your shoulders, Marsha. You didn't know what was going on, and neither did I. I should have questioned things too. I was just so happy to run this gallery with you that I wanted to believe we were doing well."

"Yes," Marsha said, smiling. "We'll figure it out together. We may have to make a few hard decisions, though, but we might just be able to save this gallery. Once I sell the Malibu house, I'll have a little extra money to keep us afloat. And then I have to decide whether to keep the Torrance insurance office or sell it to the employees. There's so much for me to deal with."

"Sell the insurance office?" Kristi looked surprised. "Won't that be your main source of income?"

Marsha shrugged. "I don't know yet. I'll have to go over the books with the accountant. Craig was preparing to sell it to the employees before he died. I have trouble believing that he'd sell it if it was a moneymaker."

"Goodness. You do have a lot to contend with," Kristi said. "I'm so sorry, hon. I wish he'd left you in a better situation."

Marsha smiled at her friend. She wished the same thing. "Well, first, let's try drumming up business by calling and chatting up our regular clients and see if we can sell some of this artwork. At least it's a start."

"I'll get right on it. Do you want to split up the list and we'll both make some calls?" Kristi asked.

Marsha wrinkled her nose and then laughed. "I can't wait."

Kristi laughed along.

Marsha and Kristi spent the better part of the next two days calling clients and telling them about the wonderful artwork available that would be perfect for their homes. The calls went well, except that everyone who Marsha called went on and on about Craig's death and how sorry they were. Many were surprised she was working so soon after the funeral. It was as if they all thought Marsha should be dressed in black and stay at home like a perfect little widow.

Marsha didn't have the luxury to do that, despite the fact of wanting to go hide away from the world.

Besides, she was proud of herself for working through her

grief by being productive. That had to count for something.

Marsha also called many of her artists to ask if they had anything new and interesting to sell at the gallery. They had always carried only the best paintings, photography, and sculptures in limited quantities because they'd wanted to be an upscale shop. But now, they needed to fill the walls and floor with as much as they dared to bring the money in.

Thursday, Marsha decided she finally had to go see the accountant about Craig's last insurance office. She had no idea how Craig spent the money from the other two offices—maybe on that other woman—but there wasn't much in their bank account so she figured it was all gone. If she could get enough from the sale of the Torrance office, she could put it away in a savings account for retirement. But then, she'd still need money to live on. It was all so upsetting to think about.

The accounting office was in a newer office building in Torrance. Thomas Kragen had been Craig's accountant for as long as Marsha could remember. He was a chief partner in the Kragen, Carter, and Johannason Accounting Firm. As soon as Marsha opened the glass door to the reception room, a nicely dressed receptionist greeted her and led her back to Tom's office.

"It's so wonderful to see you, Marsha," Tom said, standing up as she entered the room. Tom was a tall man in his fifties. He was slender with gray hair and brilliant blue eyes. Marsha always thought he looked more like a successful lawyer than the stereotypical accountant.

They shook hands, and she declined the offer of a beverage. After sitting down, Tom got right down to business.

"You asked me about the pending sale of the Torrance insurance office to the employees," he said, shuffling papers on his desk. "We had just started looking into a price for the sale before Craig passed away." He glanced at her kindly, acknowledging what a loss Craig's death was with his eyes. "I haven't looked into it any further since then."

"Can you tell me if it would be more profitable for me to keep the business rather than sell it?" Marsha asked.

"Well, that would depend on whether or not you take over your husband's current clients or spread them out to the other agents in the office," Tom said. "Do you have an agent's license?"

Marsha shook her head. She had always worked on the business end of the offices while Craig sold the policies.

"Well, then you'd either have to get your insurance license so you can maintain his client list, or you can own the agency and earn a small percentage from the commissions of the other agents' sales. Frankly, I doubt if that would be as profitable as you being an agent."

Marsha sighed. She had thought that would be his answer but wanted to make sure. "I don't really want to work in the insurance business, so I suppose it would be better to sell. Can you come up with a price for the sale of the office and let me know?"

"I'll be happy to," Tom said, smiling. "I believe that would be the best move for you. I can look at the sale of the other two offices to decide on a price. Although the Torrance office doesn't earn as much as the Monterey one did, so the price will be lower."

Marsha stood and offered her hand to shake. "Thank you, Tom. I'll look forward to your call." She turned to leave but then turned back. "By the way. Do you know why Craig sold the other two offices? And did he invest that money, or was it spent on something else?"

Tom's brows rose. "I assumed he would have discussed all this with you. I'm sorry to say, but he sold the other two offices so he could continue to live his current lifestyle. All the money went into your joint accounts. You should have access to it."

"I see." Marsha knew there was very little in her savings and checking accounts. "Apparently, I didn't pay as much attention to our money situation as I should have. Hopefully, we can sell the office for a good sum."

Tom gave her a small smile. "We'll do the best we can. I'll figure out a price and send it over to your lawyer to handle. There's no sense in getting a real estate agent involved when we can handle the sale ourselves."

"Thank you, Tom."

He nodded. Marsha walked out of the office to her car. Once inside, she forced herself not to cry.

"Why on earth didn't you tell me all this?" she asked the empty car. "Why would you leave me in such a financial mess?" So much had happened in such a short time, and it was all life-changing. She no longer had someone she could lean on and spend her life with. And her financial stability was suddenly pulled out from under her. It was all too much to take.

Without even thinking about where she was going, Marsha found herself at the cemetery and parked down the hill from Craig's grave. She had no idea why she was here, but she couldn't stop herself. Maybe if she could just stand near him and tell him how she felt, she would at least feel better.

Sighing, Marsha stepped out of her car, instantly regretting the heels she was wearing as they dug into the soft lawn. She was so intent on not tripping in her heels that she didn't see the person standing beside Craig's grave until she was almost upon her. Stopping in her tracks, Marsha gasped as she looked up into the face of the woman from the Malibu house.

"You!"

Chapter Six

Marsha stood there, hardly able to believe she was standing face-to-face with the woman who'd destroyed her life.

"I'm sorry," the woman said softly, backing away from the grave. "I didn't think you'd be here. I'll leave."

Marsha watched as the woman backed away, noting how much younger she was than her and how pretty she was, too. She was shorter than Marsha and curvy, and her long dark hair hung down her back. She had pretty brown eyes and wore little make-up. She couldn't be any more the opposite of Marsha if she'd tried.

"Were you at his funeral?" Marsha blurted out. "I don't remember seeing you there." She had no idea why she was talking to this woman, but she wanted answers.

The woman stopped and stared at her. "No. I didn't want to disturb you."

A laugh escaped Marsha's lips. "I wouldn't have known who you were if you had come. You see, I didn't know anything about you. But apparently, you knew about me."

The woman looked uncomfortable. She slipped her hands

into her jacket pockets. She looked very professional, wearing black slacks, a yellow blouse, and a striped blazer. "I'm sorry," she said again.

"Do you still work in the Malibu insurance office?" Marsha asked. The woman looked as if she'd just come from work.

"Yes. I'm an insurance agent there. I'm not an owner, though, like the others, but I earn a good living." She stood up a little straighter, obviously proud to have accomplished becoming an agent.

"I see." Marsha's eyes went to Craig's grave. The headstone wouldn't be ready for weeks, so only a small name plaque stood up from the ground to mark his grave. The flowers from the funeral still lay on the ground, most of them dead. She looked back up at the woman.

"If you knew about me, why did you continue to be with Craig?" Marsha asked her.

The woman took a step closer. "I never meant for any of this to happen," she said apologetically. "I didn't pursue him. Craig was so kind and giving. He helped me prepare for my license test and we grew close. When I became pregnant, he insisted on taking care of me. I never asked him for anything."

Marsha's heart was breaking into tiny shards with every word the woman said. Why would Craig pursue this woman when she was at home every night waiting for him? They'd never even fought. And she'd always been there for him.

"Well, you ended up pretty well off, if you ask me. A house in Malibu? Seems rather extravagant, don't you think?" Marsha's tone was cruel, but she couldn't stop herself. She hated that this woman had shared a relationship with her husband.

"The house was all Craig's idea. He wanted me and Max

to have a nice life. I never expected anything from him," she said. When Marsha only stared at her, the woman continued. "I got the letter from your lawyer. I'm searching for a place I can afford, and I hope to be out of there soon. But it's hard. I need to be near Max's school and my work, and Malibu is very expensive."

Max. The boy's name was Max. Anger seethed inside of Marsha. It was easier hating this woman and her son if she knew nothing about them.

"That's not my problem," Marsha snapped. "Craig made no arrangements for you and your son in his will. What little there is belongs to me."

The woman stared at her, but she didn't look angry. She looked defeated. Marsha would have felt compassion for her if she hadn't been her husband's mistress.

"That necklace you're wearing. The heart with the diamonds," Marsha said. "Craig gave me the exact same necklace five years ago for our anniversary. When he placed it around my neck, he said he was giving me his heart. Did he tell you the very same thing?"

The woman reached up and touched the necklace hanging there. Tears filled her eyes.

"That's what I thought," Marsha said sharply. "You see, we were both lied to." She turned away and heard the sound of the woman hurrying down the hill.

Standing there at Craig's grave, Marsha should have felt better after telling that woman off. Instead, she felt empty.

"See what you've done?" she said to Craig. "You've hurt so many people, and you've turned me into a shrew. I hope you're happy." Marsha spun around and made her way back to her car.

* * *

Marsha went home and crawled into bed. Her day had been so awful that she just wanted it to end. She cried not only for her loss but for how angry and bitter she felt. Marsha had never been a mean person, but Craig's betrayal had brought out the spitefulness in her. And she had no idea how to make those horrible feelings go away.

By morning, Marsha was exhausted. She'd slept fitfully, rethinking everything she'd said to the woman and seeing her reactions over and over again. Why had she engaged in a conversation with the woman to begin with? What had she hoped to accomplish? And why had she tried so hard to hurt the woman just because she'd been hurt? Marsha felt stupid and mean and spiteful—and she hated those feelings.

Marsha knew she should shower and go into the gallery to work, but she was so drained she just couldn't. She'd been so proud of herself for working all week and keeping her feelings stuffed below the surface. She'd thought she could work her way out of all the pain Craig had caused her. But after seeing that woman again, she knew she had to find a way to let go of her anger and bitterness. And she wasn't going to do that by working at the gallery—yet another place that reminded her of Craig's betrayal.

Marsha needed to go away.

As she sipped her coffee, she watched the sun burn off the morning fog to reveal the green-blue water. The idea of leaving for a while grew on her. Here, she was surrounded by memories. It was difficult to sort out her feelings when everything reminded her of Craig. Cleaning out his clothes and personal items hadn't taken his essence from the house. The paintings they'd chosen, the colors on the walls, and even each piece of furniture had Craig's mark on them. She needed to go somewhere that wasn't connected to Craig in any way.

Having made up her mind, she texted Kristi that she wasn't coming to work that day and then turned off her phone. She didn't want to explain herself to her friend. She just wanted to leave.

Later that day, Marsha threw some clothes in a suitcase and tossed it in the back of her car. She had no idea where she was going, but she needed to get away and clear her head.

Feeling determined, Marsha went to the bedroom to grab her purse. Turning to leave, the diamonds in the broken necklace on her nightstand winked at her. She glared at it, then snatched it up and slipped it into her pocket. She locked the house, got into her car, headed to Highway One north, and left her problems behind her.

Or so she thought.

As Marsha drove along the scenic highway, she didn't take in the beautiful views. Instead, her mind mulled over everything that had happened since Craig's death.

She knew now that he'd lied to her about going to the Monterey office since he didn't own it anymore. Instead, Craig had gone to spend a few days at the Malibu house with his son—who she now knew was named Max—and that woman.

How many times throughout the years had he lied to her? Dozens? Hundreds? Over a nine-year period, it must have been a huge number.

"You could have just left me for her," Marsha said aloud. "That wouldn't have hurt as much as finding out about all this now."

But Marsha knew it would have hurt greatly. They tried for

ten years to have a child until Craig finally told her they had to stop obsessing over it. If it happened, then he'd be thrilled, but if not, he was fine, too.

"I love you, and only you," he'd told her. "Together, we have enough to fill our lives."

Right, Marsha thought. Because by then, he had already gotten another woman pregnant and he no longer needed his wife to have a baby. He had the best of both worlds. A wife at home who adored him and a lover who'd had his child.

The pain in her heart was almost too much to bear.

On top of everything, Craig left her in a pinch for money to support herself. All these years, she thought they were doing well financially. But his having to sell two of the businesses proved they weren't. Why couldn't he have told her they were spending too much money? They'd always been a team, so why had he blocked her out?

Selling the Malibu house was a must. She couldn't afford the payments or the taxes. It had to go. And the woman in the house would have to go with it.

Marsha stewed over her problems half-way up the coast. She had thought she'd try to get to Monterey and stay in the beautiful hotel and spa on the harbor that she and Craig had stayed at many times before. But the idea of it made her stomach twist into knots. Maybe it wasn't a good idea to stay anywhere she'd spent time with her husband.

Halfway to Monterey, as she neared Pismo Beach, Marsha suddenly grew tired. All her anger had zapped her of any energy she'd had. A small billboard on the side of the road showed a beautiful, large Victorian house sitting on a hill overlooking the ocean. The Clifftop Inn Bed & Breakfast it stated in large letters. It looked charming and inviting, so when the road appeared for the inn, Marsha turned left and drove down the long, tree-lined driveway, hoping they had a vacancy for the night.

The inn was even more beautiful than the picture on the billboard. Marsha pulled her car around to the parking lot and turned it off. The large Victorian house stood three stories high with a turret on each side in the front. It was painted a soft yellow with white trim. Window boxes were filled with colorful flowers, and rose gardens sat under the windows as well. Marsha could tell it had originally been a home, but at some point, someone had added a long stretch of house in the back and extended it to add another Victorian-style building. Another addition contained a cozy-looking restaurant, which was open, and it looked like there were rooms above that. As the sun set over the ocean, warm lights glowed from the inn's windows, giving it a welcoming look.

Marsha pulled her suitcase and a smaller bag out of the trunk and rolled it down the cobblestone walkway to the entrance. There weren't many cars in the parking lot, and there were only a few people in the attached restaurant, so she hoped that was a good sign they'd still have a vacancy.

Walking through the glass and wrought-iron door into the large, tiled entryway, Marsha gazed around her. There was a staircase on one side climbing up to the second floor, a dining room on the left, and an elegant living room on the right. The entryway also had a fireplace, and a beautiful glass chandelier lit the area. It was gorgeous.

"Can I help you?" a young woman asked, standing behind a small desk straight ahead of Marsha. She smiled at the woman. She was tall and slender with dark hair and blue eyes and looked to be in her early twenties.

"Yes," Marsha said, walking up to the desk and pulling her suitcase behind her. On the wall behind the desk were several photos of the inn throughout the years. One large black and white photo showed it as only a house, probably back when it had been built. "I was hoping to rent a room for the night."

The woman smiled. "You're in luck. We have several available. Would you like a room on the first or second floor? The view on the second floor is the best."

Marsha immediately liked the girl whose name tag read Melinda. "Definitely the second floor," she said. "Do all the rooms have fireplaces?"

"Absolutely," Melinda said. "This part of the inn was built in the early 1900s by my great-grandfather. It was his house until his son turned it into an inn. Back then, all the rooms needed a fireplace for warmth. But they've been converted to gas fireplaces now."

"That's lovely," Marsha said. "Does your family still own the inn?"

She nodded. "My parents do. My mom inherited it from her parents."

Marsha loved that. A family business that was passed down through the years. It was so rare these days.

"Here's your key card," Melinda said. "You're in room 202. We have an elevator down the hallway. I can help you bring your luggage up." The girl walked around the small counter and took ahold of Marsha's bag.

"Oh, you don't have to," Marsha said.

"We always escort the guests to their rooms," Melinda said, taking the lead down the hallway.

They came to a small elevator that looked like it was built in the early 1900s.

"Don't worry," Melinda said, laughter in her voice. "It only looks old. We actually added the elevator in 2000. But my parents wanted it to fit in with the décor."

Marsha followed her inside and it only took a few seconds to reach the second floor. She then followed Melinda down the hallway and to the right to the front-facing bedroom.

"Here we are." Melinda took Marsha's key and opened the door, then allowed Marsha to go inside first.

Marsha looked around the room. It was a cozy space with a queen bed, a dresser and desk, and a small bathroom attached. Two sets of double windows flanked the brick fireplace. "It's adorable," Marsha said, turning back to Melinda. "I love it."

"Great. I hope you enjoy your stay. We serve breakfast from seven to ten each morning, and if you stay longer, you can buy lunch and dinner over at the restaurant. Of course, there are many nice restaurants in town as well."

"Thank you." Marsha reached into her purse to give Melinda a tip, but the woman waved her hand at her.

"No tip necessary. Service is all part of the price."

Well, thank you very much," Marsha said.

"Oh, and if you find you want to stay longer, let me know," Melinda said as she stood in the doorway. "We have openings all weekend and next week. It's a little slow this time of year. And if you want to walk on the beach tomorrow, there's a staircase that goes down the cliff to it. It's quite a workout but worth it."

"Thank you, Melinda."

The girl smiled and closed the door.

Marsha turned back and looked at the room. It was an absolute gem. She felt better right now than she had since Craig died.

She set her bag on a chair beside the bed and pulled out her toiletries. After placing those in the bathroom, she changed into a silky pair of pajamas and dropped onto the bed. She could read a book on her iPad, watch television, or just do nothing. How lovely was that?

Turning on her phone, she saw dozens of messages from Kristi. Marsha sighed. Kristi was worried because she hadn't heard from her. Marsha thought about ignoring the messages but felt bad about making Kristi worry. She hit her friend's number in her favorites and waited.

Kristi answered the phone on the second ring. "Marsha! I was so worried about you. I even stopped by your house after work, but you weren't there."

"I'm fine," Marsha said. "Didn't you see my text saying I was going to stay home today?"

"I did. But I was still worried. And you weren't home," Kristi said.

"Thank you for worrying, dear, but I'm fine. I decided to get away for a few days," Marsha told her. And as she looked around her room, she was so happy she had. "Since Mari and Kevin will be working the weekend, I didn't think I needed to tell you I was gone."

There was silence on the other end of the line for a moment. Finally, Kristi spoke. "I wish you had told me. I was so worried. So much has happened to you lately that it scares me when I don't know if you're safe."

Marsha was stunned by her words but even more surprised by hearing her best friend crying. "I'm so sorry, Kristi. I really am. But you don't have to worry about me. I won't do anything rash, I promise you. Yes, it's been tough these past couple of weeks. That's why I decided to get away. I couldn't think straight in my house. It has too many memories."

"I get it," Kristi said, no longer crying. "It's just," she hesitated. "Your twentieth anniversary is on Monday, and I was afraid it might have put you over the edge."

"Ah." Marsha understood now. They were supposed to have been going on a cruise the next week to celebrate their anniversary. With everything happening, Marsha had asked Jeffrey to cancel the cruise and try to get a refund. But quite honestly, Marsha had forgotten all about their anniversary being on Monday. Her mind had been miles away from that.

"I'm fine," Marsha reassured her friend. "I'm somewhere safe—beautiful, actually—and I intend on coming home soon. I just needed time to myself."

"Okay. I understand," Kristi said, sounding like her old self again. "I won't bother you this weekend. But please let me know if you need anything at all."

"You are always the first person I call, believe me," Marsha said.

They said goodbye, and Marsha collapsed on the bed. She needed this. She needed time to think without any interruption or thoughts about her predicament. And as her eyes studied the room once again, she was so happy she'd come upon the perfect place to relax.

At least for a little while.

Chapter Seven

The next morning, Marsha awoke to the smell of coffee winding its way up the stairs and the sound of the ocean on the beach below. She couldn't wait to enjoy both.

Showering and dressing in jeans and a sweater, Marsha went downstairs to the dining room, where guests were enjoying a variety of food and several choices of coffee. She placed a cinnamon roll on her plate, along with a cup of strawberry yogurt and chunks of fresh fruit, and sat at a table by the window overlooking the lush gardens.

"Did you find everything okay?" a middle-aged woman with short blond hair asked as she walked among the tables offering refills of coffee.

"Yes," Marsha said, smiling. "Are you the owner?"

"I am," the woman said. "My name is Joanna, and that handsome gentleman over there refilling the fruit bowl is my husband, Casey."

Marsha looked over by the food area and saw a tall, handsome man with dark hair.

"Our daughter must have checked you in last night," Joanna said.

"Yes, she did," Marsha said. "And she is such a nice young lady. I'm happy to meet you. I'm Marsha Winslow."

Joanna smiled. "Welcome to our inn, Mrs. Winslow. I hope you found your room comfortable."

"I did," Marsha said. She'd actually slept so soundly that the night had sped by. It was the first good night's sleep she'd had in a while. "But please call me Marsha."

"Okay, Marsha," Joanna said.

"I was thinking of extending my stay through the weekend if that's okay," Marsha said.

"That will be fine," Joanna said. "I'll put you on the schedule until Monday."

"Thank you."

Joanna left, and Marsha took a bite of a cinnamon roll which she presumed was homemade. It was heavenly.

As she ate, Marsha scanned the room and noticed that most of the guests were older couples, and one younger couple was there with their young daughter. An elderly man caught her eye, sitting in the opposite corner from Marsha. He had to be in his seventies or eighties, and he wore a brown suit with a white shirt and no tie. He reminded Marsha of one of her uncles when she was young who'd always worn a suit even when he was just visiting on a weekend.

Melinda came over to say good morning and to tell Marsha she'd booked her room until Monday. "But you can stay as long as you like," she said.

"Thank you, Melinda. If breakfast is this good every morning, you might not be able to get rid of me," Marsha teased.

Melinda laughed and went back to the desk.

After breakfast, Marsha went upstairs to get her jacket and put on a pair of sneakers. She wanted to go down to the beach and walk. She always loved doing that when Craig was on his business trips. It was her way of relaxing and clearing her head.

The morning fog had lifted and the sun was shining brightly when she walked out the front door. In front of her, Marsha was surprised to see such a beautiful garden filling the space between the inn and the cliff. There were arbors filled with trailing flowers, flower beds, and big, beautiful trees that made nice shady spots to sit under. In one garden sat an ornate metal bench. It reminded Marsha of a fairy-tale garden.

She followed the cobblestone path through the garden to the wrought-iron railing with glass inserts at the cliff's edge. To her right, she saw a set of wooden stairs that she knew would lead her down to the beach.

As Melinda had warned, it was quite a workout going down the cliff, but Marsha felt safe on the stairway. There were small landings every-so-often if you wanted to rest for a moment before continuing your descent. At each landing, Marsha stopped and took photos with her phone. The view of the ocean with the beach below was breathtaking. Marsha was used to beautiful views from her home, but this was so much more dramatic and gorgeous.

Once on the beach, Marsha walked on the sand closest to the water's edge. It was cooler down by the water and windy as it always was by the ocean. But it felt wonderful. With every step, Marsha felt like she was putting the chaos of the past two weeks behind her and forming a new beginning ahead of her.

She walked the entire stretch of the beach, then turned and headed back to the inn. By now, the family with the little girl had come down to the water as had two of the other couples staying at the inn. Marsha waved and smiled at the people as she passed them, and they returned her greeting. It was like they were all on a small, secluded island together, enjoying the peace and quiet as a small group.

The climb up the staircase was tougher than going down, but Marsha didn't mind. She stopped momentarily on each landing to catch her breath. Luckily, she was in good shape, otherwise she'd never have been able to go down in the first place. When she reached the top, she stopped for a moment to take in the view. It was glorious. Her heart felt joyful again, at least for a moment. She thought about how beauty could transform anything—even your mood.

Marsha walked slowly through the garden, gazing at each flowering plant and enjoying the large trees. The day was cool but comfortable, especially after the climb up the cliff. As she passed the small garden with the metal bench, she saw the elderly man in the suit sitting there. She smiled and waved at him, and he perked up and waved back. But she left him alone to his thoughts as she reentered the inn and went up to her room.

Marsha did something she hadn't done in ages—she took a nap. She'd left her window open a crack so she could hear the ocean waves and fell into a deep sleep. Waking up later in the afternoon, she felt refreshed. And hungry. She decided to go to the attached restaurant and have an early dinner.

"Did you have a nice walk?" Melinda asked as Marsha passed by the desk.

"I did. It's such a beautiful beach. And so private," Marsha said.

"How did you do on the staircase going down and coming back up?" Melinda asked. "It's quite a workout."

Marsha laughed. "It was, but such beautiful views. I plan on walking the beach every day that I'm here. It's therapeutic."

"I agree with that," Melinda said.

Marsha went outside as the sun fell lower in the sky over the water. She walked over to the railing overlooking the cliff and took a photo of the sun turning the Pacific Ocean orange. At home, she looked at the ocean every day and had for the ten years she'd owned the house. And she had always appreciated her lovely view. But here, it seemed even more intense and amazing. She thought how odd it was that you could see something every day and take it for granted, believing it was always going to be there. And then, one day, it wasn't.

Brushing away her morbid thoughts, Marsha turned and made her way through the garden toward the restaurant. She'd changed into a simple dress and low-heeled shoes, wearing a sweater to ward off the chill. As she walked inside the cozy restaurant, her stomach growled. She hadn't eaten since breakfast, and after that long walk and nap, she was hungry.

"Sit anywhere you wish," a tall man with blond hair and bright blue eyes said. "There are still tables by the window available so you can enjoy the view."

"Thank you," Marsha said. She chose a small booth by the window, and the man handed her a menu.

"My name is Trevor, and I'll be your server tonight," he said. "Can I get you something to drink? We have wine and craft beer, and also soda, iced tea, or filtered water."

"I'll have a glass of white wine," Marsha said.

"I'll be right back." Trevor left to go to the bar.

The place was small but nice. The lighting was soft, and there were tables and booths all around. The bar was up front, and Marsha was happy to see there were no televisions around the place. It felt like all restaurants these days had TVs running all the time, which was fine for some but distracting, too.

Marsha studied the menu. There were good, old-fashioned choices like hot roast beef sandwiches and stew, but also salads, homemade soups, hamburgers, and chicken sandwiches. The salad with grilled shrimp looked good to her and she decided to order that when Trevor returned.

"I'll put in your order," Trevor said, smiling before he walked away.

Marsha thought Trevor would be perfect for Melinda over at the inn. Then she laughed at herself. Here she was, trying to match up complete strangers.

Glancing around as she waited, Marsha noticed the place was only about a quarter full. Two of the couples from the inn were sitting in booths near her, and a couple of men she hadn't seen before were at the bar, drinking beer and eating burgers. She turned her attention to the view outside the window. Despite the lush gardens in front of the inn, a space had been left open so visitors to the restaurant could view the ocean. She watched the sun go down slowly. The colors were rich and golden. Absolutely beautiful.

Trevor brought her food, and she was thrilled to see a breadstick came along with the salad. Right now, small things made her happy. A breadstick, the sunset, a glass of wine. After all the turmoil she'd been through the past two weeks, she was relieved she could still enjoy the small things in life.

Marsha didn't mind eating alone. Craig was often on business trips, and she'd learned that if she was afraid to do things alone, she'd never do anything. So sitting in the restaurant alone, eating, didn't bother her. She didn't need a book or her phone to entertain her. Watching the sun set and enjoying the delicious food was enough.

For the first time since Craig had died, Marsha felt at peace.

Just as she was finishing her dinner, one of the other couples from the inn approached her table. They looked to be in their late 40s and were dressed nicely. Marsha hoped they didn't feel sorry for her for eating alone and wanted to join her.

"Mrs. Winslow?" the man asked quietly. "We're sorry to bother you. You're Craig Winslow's wife, aren't you?"

Marsha's heart sank. Just as she was feeling good, she was reminded of Craig. "Yes," she said.

The couple smiled. "We are so sorry about the loss of your husband," the woman said. "He was such a kind and generous man. He will be greatly missed."

Marsha was taken aback. She hadn't expected this. "Thank you. That's very kind."

"We own a business in Torrance," the man said quickly as a way of explaining how they had known Craig. "Last year, when there was so much rain, our roof leaked, and Craig came out himself to assess the damage and assure us we were covered. When the insurance company tried to pay us less, he fought for us, and we were paid in full to fix the roof. You'll never know what that meant to us."

Marsha gave them a small smile. "Yes, I do. I own my own business, too. It can mean the difference between succeeding and losing your business."

The woman nodded. "Yes. Exactly. Your husband was so kind. We also have friends who lived in the Palisades and insured their house through Craig. After those devastating fires, he fought for all his clients in Malibu and the Palisades to get them the money they deserved. He was a good man."

Marsha nodded, forcing back tears. The fires in California earlier that year had been horrendous. Craig had worked tirelessly to ensure his clients weren't canceled and they got the money they deserved. Many insurance agents couldn't say the same thing.

"Thank you both so much," she said, her voice shaking. "He was a good man, and I appreciate your kind words."

They both nodded. "We'll leave you alone. We just had to tell you how much we appreciated Craig. I hope you have a nice stay here. It's the perfect place to relax and reflect."

"Thank you," Marsha said. She watched as the couple left the restaurant and took in a deep breath to calm her shaking nerves. They were right. She'd been so angry at Craig for what he'd done that she'd completely forgotten what a good person he was.

Marsha thanked Trevor and paid her bill, leaving him a large tip, then walked out into the night toward the inn. The garden was lit with walkway lights and twinkle lights in the trees and bushes. It looked magical. But her mood had changed from uplifting to melancholy, and she didn't feel like walking the paths or going closer to the ocean to let it's sound soothe her. Instead, she headed inside to go up to her room.

When she entered the inn, she saw several couples in the living area enjoying the fire and playing cards. Melinda rushed over to greet her.

"Would you like to join us for a game of cards?" she asked, cheerful as ever.

"Not tonight, but thank you," Marsha said. "Maybe tomorrow."

Melinda nodded. "Good night," she said, then headed back into the living room.

Marsha hurried up the stairs and into her room, all the happiness of the day now gone. She dropped her purse on a chair and fell onto the bed. She knew the couple who'd approached her had only meant to make her feel good about Craig and all the good he'd done. But the effect had done the opposite. It had made Marsha feel sad and petty like she'd forgotten the whole picture of who her husband had been. All she'd been dwelling on was how he'd cheated on her for years and lied to her, and also gone through their money without telling her. Of course, she was justified in being angry with him, but she knew he'd been more than all that. He had loved her for years and cared for his clients and worked hard to help those in the community.

It was all too much to take in at once.

Instead of feeling peaceful and relaxed as she had earlier, Marsha broke down into tears about all she'd had and all she'd lost.

Chapter Eight

Marsha awoke the next morning with swollen eyes and a headache from crying herself to sleep. All the anger and sadness had come back to her, and she hated the way it made her feel. She got out of bed and took a Tylenol, then wet a washcloth with cold water and placed it over her eyes. She didn't want to go down to breakfast with swollen eyes for everyone to see she'd cried all night.

For a moment, Marsha thought she should pack up and leave and drive up to Monterey to find another place near the ocean to stay. All the good feelings she'd had about this place had deserted her last night, and she wasn't sure she could get back into that peaceful frame of mind here. But then she thought that was silly. No matter where she went, reminders of Craig would follow her. Not because the people around her remembered him but because he'd always be a part of her life no matter how far she ran.

She showered and dressed, making sure to apply her makeup carefully to cover the bags under her eyes. Then, she went downstairs to eat breakfast.

Joanna greeted her with a wave, and the couple who'd

spoken to her the night before nodded and smiled but didn't approach her. She was thankful for that. Marsha selected one of their fresh blueberry muffins and some fruit, then went to a table as far away from the other guests as possible. It wasn't that she wanted to be unsociable, she just needed time to herself.

As she ate, Marsha noticed the elderly man also sitting alone across the room. He read the newspaper while he ate, seemingly happy to be by himself. His being alone made her feel better about sitting by herself, too.

"Did you enjoy your meal yesterday at the restaurant?" Melinda asked as she carried a pot of coffee around the dining room.

"Yes, I did. And the service is great there," Marsha replied.

"That's good to hear. Did Trevor wait on you?" she asked.

Marsha nodded. "He's a nice young man."

Melinda chuckled good-naturedly. "I'll tell him you said so. He and I are engaged."

"Really?" Marsha smiled brightly. "You know, I was thinking you two would make a cute couple."

Melinda flashed her engagement ring, and Marsha reached for her hand to see it up close.

"Beautiful. He has excellent taste," Marsha said.

"Thank you. His parents own the restaurant, and we've known each other since grade school. But it wasn't until after I came home from finishing college that we dated seriously. We both love it here so much, I'm sure we'll continue the family businesses when our time comes."

"That's wonderful. You couldn't ask for a nicer business to run," Marsha said.

Melinda went off to fill coffee cups, and Marsha returned to her meal. She couldn't help but think about the young couple and the life they'd have over the next twenty years. People fall in love and marry and hope that their happiness will last a lifetime, but for many, it doesn't. Marsha had thought she was in a happy marriage for years and found out she wasn't. You just never knew what life would throw at you.

Stop being so cynical, she told herself.

After breakfast, Marsha changed into sneakers like she had the day before and wandered through the beautiful garden. The day was warmer than the day before, and there was a slight breeze from the ocean. She made her way to the staircase and walked down to the beach.

The beach was empty of people, just as it had been yesterday morning. Marsha strolled along the shoreline on the packed sand, letting her mind wander. She thought about how happy Melinda and Trevor were and how she and Craig had been the same way after they married. She wondered if they'd eventually have trouble or even stay together. Marsha had thought her marriage would last forever, and technically, it had until Craig died. She wondered, if he'd lived, how long he would have kept his secret family from her. Forever? He'd done a good job of keeping them a secret for nearly ten years. Ten years! Had she been that dumb or that trusting? Or was being that trusting being dumb, too?

She sighed.

Marsha had never had any reason to think Craig was cheating on her. She was twenty-five when they'd married, and he'd been thirty-two. They weren't children who didn't know what they were doing. Craig had already opened a successful business and knew what he wanted out of life. Marsha was a hard worker and was happy to help him build his business. They made a great team.

Craig was always attentive, kind, and sweet. He remembered birthdays, anniversaries, and other important dates. He never showed any sign of being bored with their marriage or wanting to stray. Not even during the years he had his other family. She had no reason to doubt him or suspect anything was going on. Their life had been perfect.

But now she knew it hadn't been.

Turning to walk back toward the steps, Marsha noticed she wasn't alone anymore. Two other couples were walking on the beach, and the couple with children were down there, too. She didn't see the couple who'd approached her last night, though. Maybe they'd checked out. She hoped so, because she couldn't bear to have to smile and nod again as they told her how wonderful Craig was. She agreed. Craig was a compassionate and caring human being. But they didn't know the other side of him. The side that had disappointed her.

Once up the stairs, Marsha walked through the garden toward the inn. She again noticed the elderly man sitting on the garden bench and smiled and waved to him. He waved back, then seemed to drift off into himself again. She noticed he had a cane leaning against the bench's armrest. He was definitely as old as she'd thought, and she wondered what drew him to this place. Although, the people here probably wondered the same about her. Why was this single, older woman here alone? It was human nature to wonder about others and their stories. But Marsha wasn't the nosey kind and would never ask anyone their story unless they offered it.

Feeling restless even after her long walk, Marsha decided to go into town and do some shopping. She hadn't planned well when she'd packed and needed to buy more clothes if she was going to stay here longer. So, she changed into nicer clothes and drove off down the highway to the local outlet mall.

Wandering around the many shops, she found a place to buy necessities, then went into a women's clothing shop and bought two more pairs of jeans and a couple of sweaters and blouses. Most of her wardrobe at home was dress pants and dresses with very few casual clothes. She was happy to find jeans that fit well and also bought another pair of sneakers that would be better for walking up and down the wooden steps.

Without consciously making the decision, Marsha planned on staying at the inn longer than she'd first thought. Maybe another week. Who knew? It was the perfect spot for her to hide out and figure out her life.

Marsha returned to the inn and asked Melinda if she had an available room all the next week if she decided to stay that long. Melinda smiled and nodded her head. "Definitely. Stay as long as you'd like. This place is hard to leave, isn't it?"

"It is," Marsha agreed. "It's the perfect place to relax and reflect. I'll let you know on Monday if I plan on staying."

She put her purchases away in her room, slipped on her new sneakers, and headed downstairs again. She was getting hungry, but the call of the garden was too strong, and she found herself sitting on the bench in the garden where she usually saw the elderly man. She understood the allure of the bench. It faced the ocean but was also surrounded by the scents of the many blossoming flowers. The trees shaded it from the sun, but it wasn't chilly here. The rest of the garden blocked the wind from the ocean. It was calming and peaceful.

"Do you mind if I join you?" a male voice asked, interrupting her thoughts.

Startled, Marsha looked up into the watery gray eyes of the elderly man in the suit. "Certainly. Please do," Marsha said, moving to make room for him.

He placed his cane against the armrest and, before sitting, offered his hand to shake. "I'm Andrew Trelow," he said.

Marsha shook his hand. "Marsha. It's nice to meet you, Mr. Trelow."

He chuckled as he sat. "Please call me Andrew. I'm old, I know, but I'm not that formal."

Marsha found his words funny since he was at a seaside inn, wearing a suit as he sat in the garden. He seemed formal to her. "Okay, Andrew. Are you enjoying your stay here?"

"I always do," he said, staring out into the distance. "My wife and I have been coming here every year for over thirty years."

Wife, Marsha thought. She had only seen him alone. "Is your wife with you now?" she asked.

Andrew sighed and shook his head. "No. She passed three years ago. But before she died, she told me I should continue coming here on our anniversary every year. So, I do."

"Oh, that's so sweet." His words had touched her heart. "When is your anniversary?"

"Tomorrow. The twenty-second. We were married for fifty-seven years before Irene died. That's my wife's name," Andrew said, turning to smile at Marsha. "This would have been our sixtieth wedding anniversary."

Marsha was stunned. "My wedding anniversary is on the twenty-second, too," she told him. "My husband and I would have been celebrating twenty years tomorrow."

Andrew's brows rose. "Really? Well, isn't that a coincidence? But you said it in the past tense. Did your husband pass on?"

Marsha nodded. "A little over two weeks ago. In a car accident."

"Oh, my dear. I'm so sorry. I had no idea," Andrew said.

"Thank you," Marsha said. "It was a shock to all of us."

They sat in silence for a while, enjoying the peacefulness of the garden. Then Andrew spoke up. "Would you like to join me for an early dinner at the restaurant? I just hate eating alone."

Marsha smiled. He seemed like a kindly old man, so why not? "Yes. That would be nice."

They walked slowly to the restaurant, with Marsha matching the older man's steps. When they entered, Trevor greeted them and placed them in a booth by the window.

"When we first started coming here years ago, there was no restaurant," Andrew said as he glanced at the menu. "We had to drive into town to eat dinner. That was nice, but now that I'm older, I'm glad I can stay at the inn and eat at the restaurant."

"Was the garden as beautiful then as it is now?" Marsha asked. It intrigued her that he'd been coming here for so long.

"Oh, yes. The railing along the cliff wasn't as fancy. Just an old rickety fence. And the steps going down to the beach have been greatly improved over the years." He chuckled. "You truly took your life into your hands going down that old staircase. Of course, now I no longer even try to go down there. But my wife and I walked that beach many a time."

Marsha loved imagining the good times he and his wife shared here. It was a magical place indeed. "You two must have had the perfect marriage," she said.

"Well," Andrew hesitated and looked up at her. "It wasn't always perfect. We had a few bumps along the way. But we managed to stay together happily for the long haul."

His words intrigued Marsha. Two weeks ago, she would have told anyone who asked that she and Craig had the perfect marriage. But now, she knew differently.

Trevor came to the table to bring their drinks and take their order. Andrew ordered the clam chowder and breadstick, and Marsha ordered the same shrimp salad she'd had the night before. After he left, Marsha couldn't help but ask Andrew a personal question.

"Do you mind if I ask what bumps your marriage survived?"

Andrew gave her a small smile. "If you promise not to judge me too harshly."

Marsha shook her head. "I'm the last person to judge anyone about their marriage."

Andrew nodded and glanced out the window as if the scenery would help him remember his past. "Irene and I met right after I'd served my two years in the service. I was too young for the Korean War and was lucky I wasn't sent during the early years of the Vietnam War. I'd been in the navy, and when I got out, I stayed in Southern California. I found a job as an electrician in a small appliance store, and the man who owned it had a daughter my age."

"Irene?" Marsha asked hopefully. She was already drawn into his story.

He nodded. "Yes. She worked in the store on weekends while she took classes at the local junior college. She was working on a teaching degree." He smiled brightly. "She was tiny and cute with dark curly hair and big blue eyes. I fell in love the moment I met her."

"That's so sweet," Marsha said. She and Craig hadn't experienced love at first sight, but she'd liked him the moment she'd met him.

Andrew smiled. "It was sweet. We dated, and because I was so sure she was the one, I asked her to marry me within six months of meeting her."

"Oh. How did that go over with her father?" Marsha asked.

"Her parents were unsure about it. But in those days, most of my friends were married by eighteen, so us being twenty-three seemed old." He laughed. "Her parents insisted she finish her college education even if we married, so we married in September, and she went to her second year of college. In those days, it only took two years to get a teaching certificate. I worked for her father that entire year, and we settled into a small apartment. Once she could start teaching, we moved from Long Beach to Torrance, where she found a job teaching first grade. I found a job with an electrician and worked under him until I could get my credentials to join the union. Eventually, we saved enough to buy a small house and start a family."

"So, you have children?" Marsha asked.

"Yes. Two. They, of course, are grown and married with grown children of their own. We have a boy and a girl. The perfect family."

Trevor brought their food and they each began to eat. After a few bites, Andrew spoke up again.

"Do you have children?"

Marsha shook her head slowly. "We were never blessed with children. But we wanted them. I was twenty-five when we married, and Craig was thirty-two. It just never happened."

"I'm sorry," Andrew said, then ate another spoonful of soup. "Our children and grandchildren mean the world to us. And I credit our family with keeping us together."

Marsha took a bite of her breadstick and thought as she chewed it. "Do you mind if I ask what happened?"

"I always prided myself on being faithful to my wife and putting my children first," Andrew said. "And I did both of those things for all those years. Except once." He shook his head sorrowfully.

"I'm sorry," Marsha said quickly. "I didn't mean to pry. You don't have to talk about it."

His eyes met hers. "For some reason, I feel like I should, if you'll indulge me."

She nodded.

"Our children were in their late teens, and we were in our forties. My wife returned to work as a teacher after our second child had started school, so we were a busy couple. I was running the electrician shop by then so the owner could retire. I did more paperwork than electrical work at that point. I wasn't looking to have an affair. It was the last thing on my mind. But it happened just the same. A young woman was working as the receptionist at the shop, and we got along well. Maybe too well. She was always sweet and kind at a time when my wife was so busy with the kids and her own work. I went out for an innocent dinner one night with the receptionist as a way of thanking her for working late so many nights, and, well, we ended up at her place. Believe me, I'm not proud of myself for what happened."

"Maybe we shouldn't talk about this," Marsha said, feeling uncomfortable. It felt too close to home for her.

"I'm sorry," Andrew said. "I don't want to make you uncomfortable."

Marsha closed her eyes a moment and took a deep breath. "It's my fault. I asked. The problem is it hits too close to home." She looked Andrew in the eye. "My husband cheated on me, too."

"I'm so sorry," the older man said. "I know how much I hurt my wife, and I'm sorry you were hurt."

"The worst part is," Marsha said softly. "He never admitted it to me. I found out about it after he died. It was devastating."

He nodded. "I noticed that look in your eyes. The same look my wife had for months after she found out. That's why I felt compelled to tell you my story. It might help you."

Marsha studied Andrew for a moment. Would hearing his story help her in any way? Or maybe, at his age, he needed to get that bad memory off his chest. Finally, she nodded.

"Maybe it will help," she told him. "Please continue."

Chapter Nine

Andrew nodded and took another sip of his soup. Marsha glanced around her, wondering if anyone else could hear their conversation. She didn't want anyone to hear such a personal story. But they were two booths away from another couple, and no one else was in that part of the restaurant, so she felt safe.

"I felt so guilty afterward, I just couldn't hide it from my wife. After a time, I finally confessed to having cheated on her," Andrew said. "She was angry, of course, but she was also hurt. Devastated. I could see it in her eyes. She didn't rant and rave at me, she just walked away. I moved into the guest room and she didn't speak to me for weeks. But she hadn't kicked me out, so I felt I had a chance to make it up to her."

"Did your children notice the tension in the house?" Marsha asked.

"My daughter was sixteen, and at that age, they are more into themselves, so she never questioned why I was in the guest room. My son was nineteen and in college. He had his own apartment near the school and only came home on weekends to do laundry and get a home-cooked meal."

"What happened?" Marsha asked.

"I tried talking to Irene, but she said she didn't want to hear what I had to say," Andrew said. "She told me there was no excuse. And she was right. I had no excuse because I had a loving wife at home." He shook his head. "Men are babies, really. We act like we're in charge and can handle everything that comes our way, but when we don't get all the attention we think we deserve, we stray. Personally, I couldn't rationalize why I had done it. I had no excuse. So we lived for months, barely speaking, going through the motions."

"I couldn't have done that," Marsha said. "I would have rather fought it out and get it out in the open then have that silence between us."

Andrew nodded. "I think that would have been easier. But then, when one argues, sometimes they get carried away and say things they shouldn't. So, finally, I came home one Friday night and asked Irene to pack a bag. I told her I wanted to go up north with her, find a nice hotel, and settle things once and for all. She hesitated, then finally agreed. We drove for a few hours, and that's when we saw the little billboard for this inn. We checked in, spent the night, then took a walk on the beach below the next day. It was there that she finally broke down and started yelling at me, telling me how disappointed she was and how much I'd hurt her. I think she felt safe yelling over the crashing waves so no one would hear us."

"Wow. That doesn't sound like a good first time here," Marsha said.

Andrew chuckled. "But it was. I finally knew how she felt and what I'd done to her. I preferred her yelling at me over the silent treatment. I let her yell until she was tired of it, then we came back up the stairs, sat on that very same bench in the garden, and had a long talk."

"Ah, I see now why you like that bench so much," Marsha said, smiling. "How did you get her to agree to stay with you?"

"I told her the truth. That I was stupid and inconsiderate and that I only loved her. I've always only loved her. And I begged her to forgive me. I promised her that I'd do everything possible to make her happy every day for the rest of her life. And that I'd try to never disappoint her again."

"And it worked?" Marsha asked.

"Not right away," Andrew said. "I gave Irene time to figure out if she believed me and still wanted to stay with me. I owed her that much."

"But she did come around," Marsha said. "She must have if you two spent every anniversary here after that."

He nodded. "She did. And I did my best to never give her a reason to distrust me again. I loved her that much. I would have done anything for us to stay together."

Marsha set down her fork, her salad nearly finished. "That's a lovely ending, but I don't have the luxury of forgiving or forgetting what my husband did to me. He kept it all a secret, then died and left me to pick up his mess."

"You said you were married for twenty years," Andrew said. "Were they good years or bad years?"

"Good years," Marsha said without hesitation. "But how do I forgive someone who lied to me for ten years, had another family on the side, and spent a large chunk of money that I didn't know about?"

"I agree. That would be hard," Andrew said. "I asked my wife once how she was able to forgive me and move on. She said it wasn't easy, but after a time, she said she got down to the heart of the matter. She said she looked back at all the good times we'd had and how happy we'd been, and to her, that was what mattered the most. We'd had so much love and happiness in the past, and she didn't want to throw everything away because of one mistake."

"Your wife was a good person," Marsha said. "I don't know if I have it in me to forgive and forget."

"I think we all have it in us. It just takes time." Andrew told her.

Andrew insisted on paying their bill, and Marsha thanked him.

"It's the least I could do since you had to listen to me ramble on all evening," he said, chuckling.

"I didn't mind at all," Marsha said. "I'm glad you and your wife were able to get past your indiscretion. Maybe, someday, I might be able to look back and forgive Craig for what he did."

"I hope you can," Andrew said as they walked into the inn's lobby. "Otherwise, the anger will eat you up, and you're too nice of a woman to let that happen."

"Thank you." They parted ways, with Marsha heading up the stairs and Andrew walking to his first-floor room.

All evening, Marsha thought about Andrew and his wife. It was hard not to. For him to trust her—a complete stranger—with his story was remarkable. But what had he said? He'd seen a look in her eyes that reminded him of how devastated his own wife had been. Marsha hadn't realized she'd looked as sad as she'd felt, but he'd seen it. Maybe they were meant to talk to each other. Maybe she was meant to stop at this very inn to work out her problems.

Or maybe it was all a coincidence.

The phrase that kept rolling around in her head was the *heart of the matter.* She remembered that phrase from an old

Don Henley song from the early '90s. The song continues by saying that, in the end, it's about forgiveness. If she were being honest with herself, the heart of the matter was that she and Craig had been happy. They'd shared wonderful, memorable times together. But she'd have to get past the mess he left her before she could just remember the good times.

It would take a saint to do that, and she knew she wasn't a saint.

* * *

Early the next morning, Marsha awoke on the day that would have been her twentieth wedding anniversary. She lay in bed awhile, thinking how different this day would have been had Craig not died. They would be on the Caribbean cruise right now, and he probably would have given her something amazing, like a diamond bracelet or diamond earrings. They would have eaten a delicious meal in the main dining room on board and danced the evening away under the stars.

Instead, she was alone in every sense of the word. Alone at the inn, alone in her life, alone, period.

She grabbed her phone, which had been turned off for two days, and turned it on. There were several messages from Kristi again. Marsha sighed. She knew her friend was scared to death that she'd give up on life and jump off a cliff or something. But Kristi should know her better than that. Marsha was heartbroken over everything that had happened, but she was too strong of a woman to end it all.

Marsha gave in and called Kristi.

"I was afraid you'd never call me back," Kristi said. "I was so worried about you."

"I appreciate your worrying about me, hon, but I had already told you I needed some time away. I'm still fine."

"I'm sorry," Kristi said. "It's just today's your anniversary, and I was afraid you'd be upset. I just wanted to check on you."

"I promise you that I'm fine. I've been walking on the beach and getting a lot of sleep. I really needed this after everything that's happened," Marsha said. "Please don't worry about me."

"Okay. But can you check in with me at least every few days?" Kristi asked. "Just so I won't go insane with worry."

Marsha chuckled. "I will. I'm not sure how much longer I'll stay here, but I'll text you when I head home. How is the shop doing?"

"It's fine," Kristi said. "And guess what? I sold Marco's sculpture. Our phone calls brought in clients and a gentleman who is a friend of one of our regular clients came in to see it. He bought it on the spot as a gift for his wife. They lost their house in the fires this year, and he wanted to surprise her."

"That's wonderful," Marsha said. Marsha was dealing with a lot, but she couldn't even imagine what the people who'd lost their homes to the fire had been going through. And it was a process that would last for years for some of them. "Keep it up! I'll be home soon to help, okay?"

"Okay. Please keep in touch."

"I will. And Kristi? Thank you for understanding. I really needed this time."

"You're welcome. You know I'm here for you," Kristi said.

As Marsha hung up, she realized she still had one blessing in her life—her best friend. And if she made herself stop and make a list, she knew that she had many things in her life that were good. She just needed to let go of the bad.

Finally, Marsha got out of bed and showered. She once

again thought about Andrew's story and how his wife had let go of her anger and given him a second chance. How had she done that? Did she just sweep the bad memories under the rug and keep the good ones out for all to see?

Once she was dressed, Marsha opened her small jewelry case to take out a pair of earrings to wear. Staring back at her was the heart necklace, twinkling in the light. Gingerly, Marsha lifted it from the box and studied it. She'd loved this necklace. She'd worn it every day for the past five years. But in that one instant, when she'd seen the same necklace on that woman, her beloved gift had become something she despised. The necklace now stood for everything that was wrong with her marriage and her life. Without thinking, she stuffed it into her jeans pocket, then headed downstairs to eat breakfast.

Joanna came by Marsha's table when she was almost finished eating.

"Will you be checking out this morning or staying a few more days?" she asked.

Marsha thought for a moment. She wasn't ready to go back to reality and wanted to stay a little longer. "I'll definitely stay one more night, then decide if I'll stay longer."

"Great," Joanna said. "Stay as long as you'd like." She went off to refill more coffee cups.

Marsha glanced at the guests who were eating breakfast. She didn't see Andrew this morning. Maybe he had eaten earlier and gone to his bench to reflect.

After breakfast, she walked through the garden as she'd done every day, noting that Andrew wasn't sitting in the garden. She headed down the stairs to the beach and walked along the shoreline. If she could, she'd do this every day for the rest of her life. True, she lived close enough to several beaches where she could walk in the mornings, but she preferred this one. There were no crowds, no kids surfing the waves, no distractions. She could just walk and think uninterrupted.

Finally, she turned and headed back up the stairs. Once she was at the top of the cliff, she walked to the railing and stared at the ocean view. She continued to think about what Andrew had said. Maybe letting go was easier if she got rid of the things that reminded her of Craig. She'd packed up his clothing, but that hadn't made her feel better. Maybe it was about personal items. Things that no longer brought her joy but instead reminded her of her loss.

Things like the heart necklace.

Marsha pulled the necklace out of her pocket and raised it up to the light. It twirled on the chain, sparkling in the sun. It was a beautiful necklace, but it didn't bring her joy. Looking at it brought her heartache.

If she tossed it away, would she feel better?

Closing her hand tightly around the necklace, Marsha stared out at the ocean again. She pictured throwing the necklace as far out into the blue water as she could. It would come back with the waves and crash against the rocks below, crushing it. She'd no longer have to look at it and be reminded that her husband, her beloved husband, had given this necklace to her and his mistress.

Raising her hand and pulling it back into the air, she did what she thought she had to do. She swung her arm forward, but instead of opening her fist and letting the necklace fly, she clamped it tighter. Tears filled her eyes. How could she let go of her anger if she couldn't even let go of this one reminder of his cheating?

Feeling defeated, Marsha walked back toward the inn, the

necklace still held tightly in her fist. She saw Andrew sitting on the bench, and he waved.

"Happy Anniversary," he called out as she drew close.

"Happy Anniversary to you, too," she said. "Mind if I sit?"

"Of course."

Marsha sat down and sighed. "I'm afraid the whole letting go thing will never work for me," she told him. "I thought if I let go of the thing that reminded me of the worst thing Craig did, it would free me of the memory. But I couldn't do it." She opened her hand to show him the necklace.

"It's beautiful," Andrew said. "Why would you want to get rid of it?"

"Because my husband gave this to me on our fifteenth wedding anniversary, and I cherished it. Then, I saw it on that woman—the woman he'd had the affair with. Amanda. He'd given her the exact same necklace."

"I'm so sorry," Andrew said. "That had to have been shocking. It seems you have far more to forgive your husband for than Irene had to forgive me for."

"So how do I do it?" Marsha asked. "How do I let go of my anger? How do I move on and not become a bitter old woman?"

"My dear," Andrew said gently. "It won't happen overnight. It could take months, even years. You have to give yourself some time."

Marsha sighed.

Time was something she didn't have.

Chapter Ten

Amanda

Ten years ago

Amanda DeCarlo was thrilled to have found a job. She'd been looking for a while, ever since her last job laid her off because they were closing their doors. At twenty-six, Amanda was starting her life and career over again after losing her boyfriend and job practically at the same time. But now, after a year of looking, she was hired to work as a receptionist at an insurance agency in Malibu.

Malibu!

Amanda's parents were so proud of her. Her father, Ronald, was a plumber, and her mother, Rena, had worked for years as a salesclerk in a large department store. Amanda had been the first in the family to go to college and get a degree—even if it was only a two-year business degree. She'd started a job immediately out of college for a large business supply company as a receptionist with a chance to become a sales representative, but two years later, both she and her boyfriend of nearly two years were laid off when the company closed down.

Amanda had applied everywhere from banks to offices and even in the many stores in their area, but she was either too qualified or not qualified enough. And being such a large town, there were hundreds of applications for every job. Soon, her unemployment insurance ran out, and her boyfriend found a job in San Francisco. Amanda thought about following him there but wasn't completely sure about moving so far away. Finally, she said goodbye to her boyfriend and ended up moving home—back to where she'd started four years before.

And then she widened her search and found her new job.

Of course, that meant finding something affordable to rent as close to Malibu as possible, which wasn't easy. After searching, she found a tiny studio apartment on the edge of Santa Monica, and even though she would still have a long drive to work, she didn't mind.

From the very first day, Amanda knew she was going to like working at Craig Winslow's Insurance Agency. The owner, Mr. Winslow, was an older gentleman who always wore a suit and was professional but friendly. She remembered the managers at her last place of employment barely even looking at staff on a lower level than they were, let alone talking to them. But Mr. Winslow—he said to call him Craig, but she had trouble doing that—treated everyone equally.

The staff at the agency included Walter Carson, a middle-aged man who was nice and was both an agent and the office manager, Gerald Rameriz, a younger man who dressed a bit more casually but was always smiling, and Andrea Simms. Andrea had been the receptionist before Amanda was hired but had studied and passed her insurance exam and was a new agent there. She helped Amanda the most since she knew the receptionist job well.

"You'll do great here," Andrea said. She was medium height with short brown hair, warm brown eyes, and an infectious smile. "You're pretty and sweet, and people always feel more comfortable when they are greeted by a friendly receptionist."

Amanda had appreciated Andrea's compliment, but she didn't believe she was pretty compared to Andrea. Amanda was shorter and curvier, with an olive complexion and dark hair and eyes. Despite always trying new diets and exercise programs, she never felt she was ever thin enough or pretty enough. But she did know she was a good worker and she prided herself on that.

"And you know you can always study to become an insurance agent in your free time," Andrea told her. "It takes a while unless you have loads of free time, but it's worth it. I just started, and Craig handed over a few of his own clients to me to get going. It was so generous of him. I can make money right away while I build my client base."

Amanda thought working toward becoming an agent was a good idea. But first, she had to master the flow of this particular office.

After a few weeks of working there, Amanda felt comfortable doing her job. She answered the phone, made appointments, sent out mailings, greeted customers, and did a lot of data entry work. But that was good. She was learning the terms and procedures for selling insurance policies from all the data entry. She also learned Craig's schedule by heart. His main office was in Torrance, but every two weeks, he drove to Monterey to check on that office and then stayed a day or two in Malibu to spend time in this office.

She wondered if his wife hated those weeks when he was

gone or if she was just used to it. She knew he was married, because of the picture of his wife on his desk and from how much he spoke about her. Craig was a loving and attentive husband—there was no doubt—and that was one of the many things she admired about her employer.

After three months of working there, Craig called her into his office one Thursday afternoon.

"How are you liking your job here?" he asked Amanda. Craig had the largest office in the building, with big windows that looked out toward the ocean. He sat behind his desk, his suit jacket hanging over the back of his chair and his tie loosened.

"I love working here," Amanda said eagerly. "Everyone has been very helpful and kind. Andrea said I picked up the job quickly."

Craig smiled. "That's wonderful. I knew the moment I met you that you were a go-getter. And I know you are working hard. Are you interested at all in becoming an agent someday?"

Amanda's heart beat faster. She would love to study to become an agent. But she'd looked online to see what she'd have to do, and the course work and tests were expensive. "I am interested," she told him. "But I'm afraid the cost is out of my reach right now."

"Well, that's the benefit of working for me," Craig said. "I'll be happy to pay the fees if you want to take the classes. All I ask in return is that you work for us for two years after earning your license. After that, you can move to another agency or go out on your own if you wish."

Amanda was stunned. They'd actually pay for her class materials? "That sounds wonderful," she said. "Where do I sign?"

Craig chuckled. "No signature needed. I trust you. So far, I've found most people who I've helped get their license stay with us. Tell me when you're ready, and we'll buy you the class materials."

"I'm ready now," Amanda said. "I had wanted to move up in my old job, but then they closed their doors. I'm anxious to work toward a better future."

"That's great," Craig said. He opened his top desk drawer and pulled out a credit card. "Have Andrea show you the website and help you choose the classes you need. You can put it on this credit card." He stood and handed her the card. "I'm thrilled we'll have a new agent here soon."

Amanda stood and took the card. She was so excited, she wished she could hug him, but she knew that would be inappropriate. "Thank you so much. I couldn't have done this without your help."

"You're very welcome," Craig said. "I'm always happy to help someone move up in the world. I've been so blessed; I want to be able to use my resources to help others."

Amanda felt she'd been blessed, too. Fate had led her to this good job and this generous man. She was on her way to becoming successful.

* * *

Amanda soon learned that wanting to be successful and doing the work to get there were two different things. Andrea helped her sign up for the online classes and buy the class materials. After that, it was up to Amanda to do the work and pass the tests. So, at night, after a full day of work, she sat down at her computer and took the online classes. She worked on the workbooks and studied the materials. Sometimes, she asked Andrea for help when she didn't understand something. Andrea, Walter, and even Gerald helped her by explaining important topics that were confusing or calculations that she didn't quite understand. They even gave her hints of what might be on the test and what to study for. Each test cost money to take, so she did the practice tests several times so she knew the material backwards and forwards. Still, even though she knew she was smart enough to learn all of this material, it sometimes got the best of her.

Late one Thursday afternoon, Amanda was going over her test materials and feeling like a failure. There were no more appointments for the day and she'd finished her data entry, so she was studying her work. But she was so frustrated. It just couldn't be that hard!

Each of the agents said goodbye to her for the night as they walked out the door. Soon, Craig came out with his coat and briefcase in hand.

"Oh, are you still here?" he asked Amanda, looking surprised. "Everyone is gone. You might as well go home, too."

Amanda looked up, surprised she'd stayed this late. "Sorry," she said, piling all her workbooks together to leave. "I hadn't realized it was getting late."

Craig chuckled. "Not a problem. How are you getting along with your classes?"

"Okay," she said without much enthusiasm. "I'm studying the material, but my brain doesn't want to retain it."

Craig set his coat and briefcase down and leaned against her desk. "Don't let it get you down. It's a lot of information to learn all at once. Give yourself some time to let it sink in."

Amanda looked up at his kind face, pushing a stray strand

of hair away from her face that had fallen out of her ponytail. She always wore her long hair up because she thought it looked more professional, and, with her baby face, older. "What if I can't learn it? Maybe I'll only be a receptionist for the rest of my life."

Craig shook his head. "You know that isn't true. I've seen you work around here. You pick things up quickly and never need to be told twice how to do something. You're smart."

Amanda wrinkled her nose, not quite believing what Craig was saying.

"Amanda," Craig said. "You know all that data entry you do? It has codes and figures on every sheet, right?" He waited until she nodded. "It takes most people a long time to figure out those codes and type them in correctly, yet as far as I've seen, you picked it up quickly. No one has complained that you've made any mistakes. Do you know how rare that is?"

Amanda was surprised by this. It all seemed so easy to her. "Really? Or are you just trying to make me feel better?"

Craig smiled. "It's true. Between you and me, Andrea took a long time to do the data entry flawlessly. She was here two years before she passed the test to become an agent. You've been here, what? Five months? And I'll bet you're almost ready to take the test."

Amanda smiled back. "That does make me feel better. And yeah. I'm hoping to try to complete the practice test in a couple of weeks."

"See? You're a natural. Why don't you get your things, and I'll walk you to your car?"

Amanda placed her books and workbooks into a canvas bag and followed Craig out the door. He walked with her to her car in the small parking lot. The office sat on a hill above

Malibu and was up just high enough to see the ocean over the houses that lined the Pacific Coast Highway. "I'll never get over this view," Amanda said. "I still can't believe I work in such a beautiful place."

Craig looked over at the view and sighed happily. "I never get tired of this view. My wife, Marsha, and I recently purchased a home in Palos Verdes overlooking the ocean. We love it. It was her dream house."

"That would definitely be my dream home," Amanda said. "But I doubt I'll ever own anything that luxurious."

Craig gave her a long look. "Never say never, Amanda. Always reach for the stars."

Amanda nodded and got into her car. She waved at Craig and drove away toward her little apartment. She hoped Craig was right. Maybe someday, Amanda would have everything she wanted. She'd just keep working hard and do the best she could.

Chapter Eleven

Amanda

Three weeks after her uplifting conversation with Craig, Amanda passed the insurance test. Once it was verified, she'd be a licensed agent.

Everyone in the office was thrilled for her. She'd been gone that Friday morning for the test, and when she came into work, they all cheered and hugged her.

"We all have to go out and celebrate," Craig said. "My treat. The restaurant at the hotel I'm staying in is excellent. Let's go there after work."

Everyone agreed it was a great plan. Craig told them to feel free to invite their spouses and significant others. Walter was married, and Gerald had a live-in girlfriend. But neither Andrea nor Amanda were seeing anyone special, so they showed up alone.

Craig always stayed in a five-star hotel right on the ocean when he visited the office. It was the type of place that only the uber-rich could afford. When Amanda walked into the lobby, she was spellbound. She'd never seen a place so lovely with a view so spectacular.

"Incredible, isn't it?" Andrea asked her as they waited for everyone else to arrive. "And he can afford to stay here by being an insurance agent. Although," she grinned. "Craig owns three offices in high-income areas, so I suppose he makes much more money than I ever will. But a girl can dream."

Amanda didn't even dream of places like this. She knew she'd never make the kind of money needed to stay here.

Craig finally showed up along with Walter and his wife, Susan, and Gerald and his girlfriend, Anita. They all walked toward the restaurant with Amanda falling behind next to Craig.

"Don't you usually go home on Friday night?" she asked Craig. "Won't your wife miss you?"

Craig smiled. "There was no way I was going to miss out on celebrating your big day. Marsha will understand. She knows how much we need new agents to stay in business. Besides, she's been busy running the Torrance office and fixing up our new house. I'll be home in time tomorrow to help with the yardwork she wants done."

Once seated at a table with a view of the ocean, Craig ordered a bottle of champagne for the table as well as both red and white wine. After they ordered their meals—at prices that stunned Amanda—they poured champagne all around and toasted Amanda.

"To our newest insurance agent," Craig said, raising a glass. "And to a long, prosperous career."

"Cheers!" everyone said, clinking glasses.

They all talked and ate their delicious meals, laughing and enjoying this casual time together. Andrea kept refilling Amanda's glass with champagne even when Amanda shook her head and said she'd had enough.

"Oh, come on. Enjoy!" Andrea said. "You're beginning a whole new phase in your life. Celebrate it!"

Amanda wasn't much of a drinker, and the alcohol went to her head quickly. She ate the bread that had been put on the table to try to soak it up, but with each sip, she knew she was getting drunker. But she didn't want to stop. She was having so much fun with this new family of co-workers she'd gotten to know over the last eight months. And Andrea was right. She'd worked hard to pass her test, and she deserved a night out.

Everyone was acting silly by the time they'd all finished their dinner. Craig seemed tipsy and even serious Walter was three sheets to the wind. Luckily, his wife had drunk very little, and Gerald's girlfriend had been careful, too, so the women could drive their men home.

Andrea and Amanda stumbled to the ladies' room to freshen up before leaving.

"Ugh! I've had too much to drink," Andrea said. "There's no way I can drive home."

"Me too," Amanda said. "I'd better call an Uber."

When they returned to the table, Craig was retrieving his credit card from having paid the bill.

"Let us drive you home, Andrea," Susan said. "You don't live too far from us."

"Oh, that's great. Thanks," Andrea said.

"What about you, Amanda? Do you need a lift?" Gerald asked.

"I don't live near you," Amanda said, swaying where she stood. "I'll have to call an Uber."

"Will they drive you to your place?" Andrea asked. "You live like forty-five minutes from here."

Amanda shrugged, glancing at her phone. She was searching for the app.

"I'll make sure she's safe," Craig told the group. "Maybe she can get a room here for the night."

Amanda looked up quickly from her phone. "I can't afford that," she said.

The others laughed. "It's probably the same price as an Uber to your house," Gerald said. "Just don't drive, okay?"

Craig walked everyone out to the lobby and waved goodbye. He'd be leaving the next morning to go home. Once the rest of the group had left, he turned to Amanda. "Let me rent a room for you. I'll pay for it. I'd feel safer doing that than letting you ride home with a stranger."

By this time, Amanda had given up on opening the Uber app on her phone. She was way drunker than she'd thought. "I can pay you back," she said.

Craig laughed. "Don't worry. Better safe than sorry." He linked arms with her to steady her, and they walked to the front desk. "Do you have any rooms available tonight?" he asked the woman working there.

"Of course, Mr. Winslow. Let me look."

The hotel clerk made up two key cards for the room and handed them to Craig. "It's room 240," she said. "Let me know if you need anything."

"Thank you," Craig said.

By this time, Amanda felt sleepy. She'd moved closer to Craig and placed her head on his shoulder. Craig held her tightly and walked her over to the elevator.

"You have to stay awake long enough to get to your room," he told Amanda, chuckling.

Amanda lifted her head. "Thank you so much, Craig," she

said. "You're such a nice man. Why can't I find someone as nice as you? All the men my age are stupid."

Craig laughed as the elevator stopped and opened up on the second floor. "I guess some men have a lot of growing up to do."

He walked her to her door and then opened it with the keycard. "Will you be okay?" he asked her, handing her the little envelope that held both keys. "Maybe we can meet for breakfast tomorrow morning before I leave."

"Okay. Thanks, Craig." Amanda pushed on the door and walked one step before her heels tripped on the tile entryway. Craig rushed to her side before she fell onto the floor.

"Come on. I'll help you inside," he said. He walked her to the chair by the bed and had her sit down. Then he knelt down and slipped off her high-heeled sandals. "There. Now, you won't stumble when you walk."

Amanda sat there, staring down at him. "You're like my prince charming," she said, slurring.

Craig stood. "Hardly." He smiled. "I'm just a middle-aged insurance agent."

"No, you're not," Amanda said, standing up. She was a full head shorter than him. She gazed up into his warm, brown eyes. "You've been nothing but kind to me. And encouraging. Thank you for everything you've done for me." She reached up, wrapped her arms around his neck, and hugged him tightly.

"You're very welcome, dear," Craig said, gently pulling away from her. "And you're too pretty, and we're much too drunk to be in this room together alone. Get some sleep, and I'll see you in the morning." He tried turning away, but Amanda grabbed his hand. Craig turned back to her.

"Please stay," Amanda whispered, standing up on tiptoe to kiss him.

"I really should go," Craig said softly.

"Stay." And she pulled him close again.

* * *

The next morning, Amanda awoke with a dry mouth and questionable stomach. She slowly looked around, trying to remember what had happened last night. Suddenly, her eyes widened as it all came rushing back to her.

"Oh, God," she whispered. What had she done?

Her dress and heels were lying on the floor in a puddle next to the bed, and she had nothing on. She looked around the room, but no one else was there.

Did she dream what had happened?

The clock by the bed said it was eight a.m. Slowly, she got out of bed, found her panties and chemise, and headed for the bathroom. She desperately needed a shower to help her wake up.

Later, she had showered and was wearing the hotel's cotton robe when there was a knock on the door. She hesitated. Her hair was wrapped in a towel, and she knew she looked terrible.

"Amanda? I brought coffee," Craig's voice called from the other side.

Holding her breath, Amanda knew she couldn't hide from Craig forever. She worked for him, for Pete's sake! What had she done? She cracked the door open, and there stood Craig, looking fresh in a polo shirt and slacks, holding a tray with pastries and coffee cups on it.

"Hi," Amanda said as she let him in. Despite everything,

she was hungry and needed coffee.

"Good morning." Craig carried the tray in and set it on the table beside the window. "Mind if I open the drapes?"

"No. Go ahead." Amanda ran over to where her dress was still on the floor and picked it up. Maybe she should get dressed before eating anything.

"Come sit and enjoy the coffee and the view," Craig said. "Everything is better with an ocean view."

She walked over to the table and saw that Craig was right. The room faced the ocean, and it was gorgeous. Sitting down, she took a turnover from the tray and accepted the coffee from him.

"A teaspoon of milk and two sugars, right?" Craig asked.

Amanda nodded. "How do you know how I like my coffee?"

"I pay attention," Craig said. "How are you feeling today?"

Amanda wondered if he meant how she felt after drinking too much or after what happened between them. "A little queasy, but fine."

He nodded. "About last night," Craig began, but Amanda interrupted him.

"Don't worry about it. It's fine."

Craig frowned. "Is it fine? I mean, you seem really nervous this morning."

Amanda let out a long sigh. "Honestly, I don't know if I dreamed what happened or if it happened."

"I see." Craig looked thoughtful. "Well, if we're being honest, I'm not sure what to say either. We were both too drunk last night to have made a logical decision, and I, as your boss, should have been the one to walk away. I've been worried all morning that you'd think I took advantage of you and our situation last night, but then I tell myself that maybe I did. I just hope you didn't feel like I forced you into anything."

"No, not at all. I was afraid of what you'd think of me."

They stared at each other for a moment.

"So, you're not mad at me?" Craig asked.

She shook her head. "No. If I remember right, I asked you to stay."

Craig looked down at his hands. His gold wedding ring twinkled in the light from the window. "Well, I'm mad at myself." He looked up at her. "I've never cheated on my wife in all the years we've been married. I love her very much. But now, I can't make sense of why I didn't walk away last night."

Amanda felt bad for him. Everything from last night was swirling around in her head. Andrea kept refilling her champagne glass. No one lived close enough to where she lived to drive her home. All Craig was doing was trying to keep her safe when he rented the room for her. He wasn't even going to walk into the room with her until she'd stumbled.

She was the one who'd insisted he stay with her.

"Everything is okay," she said. "It was something that just happened. We're two grown people. It's not like we're going to let it happen again."

"I'm sorry, Amanda. I mean, you're such a pretty girl and so very smart. You deserve someone younger who you can have a family with. I didn't mean to cross any lines last night, and I wouldn't blame you if you thought badly about me."

"No. I don't think badly about you," Amanda said. "I know you're a nice man. Look at all you've done for me." She hesitated, suddenly scared she may have ruined her future. "I'll still be able to work at your office, won't I?"

Craig looked surprised. "Of course, you'll still work there. I just hope I won't make you feel uncomfortable after this."

She smiled. "I can forget about it if you will."

Craig suddenly looked sad again. "I'm not sure I'll ever forget about last night. But I will do everything I can to make sure you feel comfortable working around me."

Amanda studied Craig's face as he turned to look at the view. Did he have feelings for her? He seemed so upset about cheating on his wife. "We can still be friends as well as co-workers," she said.

Craig turned back to her. "Yes. We can. You're a sweet girl, Amanda."

She gave him a small smile and started eating her turnover. She believed they could have a working relationship even after last night.

Three months later, Amanda realized she was pregnant.

Chapter Twelve

Amanda

When the drugstore pregnancy test came up positive, Amanda was stunned. She knew she had been feeling strange. She'd been sick in the mornings, and the smell of coffee turned her stomach, along with eggs and even toast. At first, she'd thought she had a mild flu. But now, she knew the truth.

And she knew exactly who the father was.

After the night in Malibu, she and Craig had been able to maintain a normal working relationship and friendship. Craig had remained friendly but had not crossed any lines. Yet she knew if she'd gone to him with any problems, he would have been more than happy to help. He was just that kind of person. Along with Andrea and Walter, Craig had helped her start building her client list. Everyone had been generous with their time and in letting her take on the new walk-in and call-in clients. They all wanted her to succeed because that helped the agency to succeed.

She wondered how disappointed everyone would be with her when they found out she was unmarried and pregnant.

And she worried about what her parents would think, too. Her parents were devout Catholics, and they hadn't liked it when she'd lived with her boyfriend without being married. To try to explain to them that she was pregnant from a one-night stand would be difficult. But to say she was pregnant by her married boss would be unthinkable.

Amanda wasn't sure what she should do. Quit her job and move somewhere no one would know her? Tell Craig? Terminate the pregnancy and tell no one? That option weighed heavily on her mind. She didn't like the idea of an abortion. But now, faced with a pregnancy, she was actually thinking of it as a viable option.

Each day at work was torture. She worried about her dilemma constantly. If she decided to terminate the pregnancy, she knew she'd have to do it soon. But each day when she woke up, she couldn't bring herself to make that difficult decision.

On a Friday afternoon, when only she and Craig were left in the office, Amanda drew up all her courage and walked into his office.

"Do you have time to talk?" she asked.

Craig smiled up at her, but when he saw the pained look on her face, his smile fell. "Of course. Always."

Amanda sat in one of the chairs facing his desk. She didn't know how to tell him. She didn't want him to think she'd use it against him.

"Whatever you have to say, please say it," Craig said gently. "Are you leaving us for another job? Have you been sick? I know something has been wrong."

Amanda closed her eyes and let out a big sigh. "No. None of those things. It's worse." She lifted her head and stared into Craig's eyes. "I'm pregnant."

Craig's eyes widened. "You are? Really?" He looked stunned.

"Yes. Over three months. Craig," Amanda said. "You're the father."

Craig sat up straight in his chair, his eyes wide. "I'm the father?" he asked softly. "Really? I can hardly believe this."

"I haven't been seeing anyone else before or since you and I spent that night together," Amanda said quickly. Was he going to deny he was the father?

"Oh, no. I wasn't saying you were lying," Craig said, looking apologetic. "I'm just in shock that you're pregnant with my baby. My wife and I have tried so hard to have children. I thought I might have been the problem," he stopped talking. "I'm sorry. I'm just trying to process all of this."

"I don't know what to do," Amanda said, tears forming at the corners of her eyes. "My parents will be devastated that I'm single and pregnant. It will change my entire life." She looked at Craig. "You need to help me decide if I should keep the baby or terminate the pregnancy."

"Terminate?" Craig looked stunned. He stood and walked over to her, then fell to his knees and held her hand. "I know it's not my place to tell you what to do. Do you want this child?"

Tears rolled down her face. "I don't know. I don't earn enough money to care for a child properly, and my apartment is so tiny. And what about daycare? How could I ever afford that? But I also don't want to lose this baby either. I don't know what to do."

Craig stood and offered his hand. "Let's go to the breakroom where we can sit and talk. Or, we could go out and eat somewhere," he offered.

She shook her head. "I don't want anyone to overhear us. If anyone knows I'm carrying your baby, it would do more harm to you than to me."

He nodded and led her to the breakroom at the back of the office. It had a small kitchen with a coffeemaker and refrigerator and two tables with chairs. Amanda sat in one of the chairs, and Craig moved a chair closer to her and sat down.

"We have to think this through. Together," he said. "What do you want to do?"

"I don't know," Amanda said. "This is all I've thought about for days. No matter what I choose, my life will change forever. My parents will disown me if I keep the baby. But I couldn't live with myself if I don't keep the baby."

"Then you have your answer," Craig said gently. "The only person who matters is you. You just said it; you couldn't live with yourself if you terminated this pregnancy. You have to keep the baby."

Amanda thought about it for a moment and realized he was right. She'd been so worried about what everyone around her would think, but how she felt was the most important thing. She raised her eyes to his. "How do you feel about that?"

"You keeping the baby?" He smiled. "I think it's wonderful. If that's what you want to do, I promise I'll do everything possible to make you and the baby's life comfortable. I won't abandon you." His smile faded as he hesitated. "But my wife can never know. It would kill me if she left me."

"So we both have a lot to lose no matter what I decide," Amanda said softly.

Craig stood and walked over to the fridge, taking out two bottles of water. He handed one to Amanda, then opened one for himself and drank from it. "This is happening to you, and I'll respect any decision you make. But my offer of help is real. I will make sure you and the baby are always safe and cared for."

Amanda knew she wanted the baby. She was single and twenty-seven with no serious relationship. Who knew when she'd ever find someone she loved enough to have a child with. And she couldn't terminate this pregnancy. She already loved this child growing inside of her. "Will you be able to keep this big of a lie from your wife and be able to live with yourself?" Amanda asked.

"I'll have to," Craig said, sitting down and running his hand through his hair. "She'd be devastated if she knew. But I can't turn my back on you, either. Our child will mean the world to me."

Amanda took a deep breath and let out a long sigh. If she kept this baby, they would both pay dearly for it. But it was a risk she had to take. She wanted this baby.

"What should I tell everyone at the agency?" she asked. "They'll think I'm terrible."

Craig shook his head. "No, they won't. Everyone here already adores you. They'll just think that these things happen, and they'll all rally around you. I know they will."

"My parents will disown me. My brother, Ryan, too. He's twenty-four and engaged to be married. He's doing everything right," Amanda said sadly.

Craig reached for her hand and squeezed it. "I'm so sorry this happened to you. It's all my fault. I should have been the strong one and walked out of your room that night. I'm so, so sorry."

"It was both of our faults, not just yours. I know I asked you to stay." Amanda said. She'd remembered it despite all that she'd drunk. And she couldn't say she hadn't wanted something to happen between them. Craig was always so kind and sweet. Who wouldn't have wanted to be with him? She couldn't let him take all the blame.

"I won't let you down, I promise," Craig said. "I'll take care of you."

"I believe you," Amanda said. "I can't go through this without your help."

And Craig kept his promise.

At five months pregnant, Amanda couldn't hide her pregnancy from her co-workers any longer. She was too short-waisted to get away with hiding it. And she knew that everyone had noticed she'd put on weight but were too polite to say anything. She finally told Andrea that she was pregnant.

"Oh, my goodness!" Andrea said, clapping her hands together happily. "Congratulations!"

Amanda was surprised by her reaction. "There's no father involved, though. It's just going to be me."

"Oh." Andrea's smile faded. "I'm sorry. What a creep! Leaving you to do this all alone. Well, don't you worry. Your work family will be behind you one hundred percent." She hugged Amanda tightly.

Amanda let her think the guy had deserted her. It was easier than trying to come up with a lie. She also knew that Andrea would quietly tell everyone else what had happened, and soon enough, they'd all rally around her.

She wished it would be that easy with her family.

On a Saturday, she drove to her parents' house in Torrance and sat down with her mother and father. She could tell by the look on their faces they'd already guessed what she was going to tell them.

"I'm sorry to disappoint you two," Amanda said after telling them she was expecting a baby. "I know you'd rather me be married first. But it happened, and there's nothing I can do now."

"Won't this man step up and at least help you?" her father, Ron, asked, frowning. "It's the least he could do."

"He doesn't know," Amanda said. "And I don't want him to be in my life. He wasn't someone I was in love with. It won't help for him to be involved."

Her mother, Rena, shook her head and cried.

"I'm sorry, Mama." Amanda was also crying. "I've tried to be a good daughter. But even I make mistakes."

Her mother stood and hugged her then. "We are always here for you, dear. I just have to get used to the idea. But I'm thankful you decided to have the child. You did the right thing."

Amanda was relieved that her parents didn't kick her out of the house.

"You need to move home so we can help you," Ron said. "We can fix up your room as a nursery, and you can have Ryan's old room."

"That's sweet of you, Papa, but my job and life is in Malibu. I earn enough money to take care of myself. And my job allows me to work at home when I need to," Amanda said. The last thing she needed was to live with her parents. She knew that Craig would want to see the baby regularly and he couldn't if she lived at home.

"Don't be silly. Who'll babysit? Who'll help you?" Ron said. "We can take care of you."

Amanda hugged her father. "I know you can. But I need to take care of myself. This is my life, Papa. I need to make my own decisions and take care of the baby on my own."

It took some persuasion before her parents stopped insisting she move home. Amanda was thankful they still loved her and wanted her to come home. But she knew she had to continue living her life independently.

Of course, with a little help from Craig.

When she was eight months pregnant, Craig rented a two-bedroom condo for her closer to Malibu. At first, Amanda resisted the idea of living in a home he paid for. But when she saw it, she couldn't say no. It was so much nicer than her apartment and in a much safer area. She would be only minutes from work, too.

"I agree it's a better place to live," she told Craig. "Thank you for doing this. But I'll pay all the bills, and as soon as I can afford my own place, I'll move out."

"You do what you have to do," Craig said. "But please let me help when I can. I want to be a part of this child's life if you'll let me."

"There's no doubt you'll be a part of his or her life," Amanda said. "It may be a bit confusing when the child is older that you and I were never married, but I want our child to know their father."

Craig hugged her. "Thank you. I know I won't have any rights, so I appreciate you being open to me being around when I can."

Amanda attended birthing classes with Josie—her brand-new sister-in-law who she'd known since her brother Ryan was in high school—as her coach. Josie was a dark-haired beauty who'd recently married Ryan after years of dating. She was excited to help Amanda and be there when the baby was born.

In some ways, Amanda was sad that Craig wouldn't be there on the day his child was born. But it also would have been awkward. Even though they'd had sex that one time, they'd been more like friends or close co-workers ever since, and she wouldn't want him watching her doing something as intimate as giving birth.

She knew it was a strange situation.

On a Wednesday afternoon in October, Amanda was talking to a client on the phone when she felt pressure on her stomach. After ending the call, she stood, thinking she'd sat too long and needed to stretch her muscles. But after another minute, her stomach felt odd again, like it was tightening up, then slowly letting go. Knowing she was due to have the baby any day now, she wondered if this was the first stage of labor.

Amanda sat back at her computer and looked up contractions. Even though she'd taken the classes, she still had no idea what it would feel like. She read descriptions online of other women's experiences with the first stage of labor.

This could be it.

"Are you in labor?" Andrea asked, coming up behind her. She'd seen what was on Amanda's computer screen.

"I don't know. It feels weird, though," Amanda said. Suddenly, a pang hit her hard. Amanda sucked in her breath until the pain subsided. She turned to Andrea. "I guess I am."

"Oh, my goodness!" Andrea exclaimed. "We need to get you to the hospital."

Craig had just come into the office after driving up to Malibu that morning. He stopped in the hallway and looked at Amanda. "Is the baby coming?"

Amanda nodded but then winced when a new pain came.

"The contractions are coming fast," Andrea said excitedly. "Come on. I'll get you to the hospital."

"I'll drive her," Craig said calmly. He still had his briefcase in hand and had just come from his car. "Why don't you follow us there."

Andrea nodded and ran to get her things. By then, Walter

and Gerald had come to see what all the fuss was about.

"Good luck," they both called out as Craig held onto Amanda to escort her to the car. "Call us when the baby is born."

Craig helped Amanda into his car. Luckily, his Mercedes was large enough for her to slip into the seat easily. As she sat, another contraction began. Craig held her hand, and Amanda squeezed it until the pain subsided.

"Sorry," she said sheepishly. "I didn't mean to crush your hand."

Craig laughed. "I'm fine. You're the one in pain. I'll get you to the hospital quickly."

Amanda called her sister-in-law and told her to meet her at the hospital—fast! She called her parents too. They were forty-five minutes away. Both said they'd come immediately.

Ten minutes later, Craig pulled up to the hospital entrance and helped Amanda out. Andrea had arrived a couple of minutes earlier and had run inside for a wheelchair.

"Here you go," Craig said, helping Amanda sit in the chair. "I'll park and wait for news in the waiting room. He locked eyes with Amanda, and she smiled back at him. She knew he was both excited and worried despite his calm demeanor.

"Let's get you inside," Andrea said. She pushed her inside, and Craig left to park his car.

Andrea texted him a moment later asking him to take care of the insurance information for Amanda. "They want to take her up to a room immediately."

He texted that he would. When he entered the hospital, he went to the front window. "I'm here to give you information for Amanda DeCarlo's check-in."

The young woman behind the desk frowned. "Are you her husband?"

"No," he said, chuckling.

"Father?" the woman asked.

"Wrong again. I'm her employer. I have the insurance information right here."

Craig sat in the far corner of the small waiting room and checked his phone for messages. He was trying to stay calm, but his heart was beating fast. He was going to be a father. How he wished he could be there when the baby was born, but that would be awkward for Amanda. They didn't have a physical relationship, so he didn't belong in the room. But he was still going to have a child, and that excited him.

His phone buzzed, and he saw it was a message from Marsha. In all the excitement, he'd forgotten to text her that he'd made it safely to the Malibu office. *"Sorry,"* he texted. *"One of our agents had a medical emergency, and I had to drive her to the hospital. I'm safe and sound."*

Marsha texted back that she hoped the employee would be fine, and Craig assured her she would. He didn't like lying to Marsha. She was a wonderful wife and partner in life. He knew she'd never have lied to him. But he couldn't tell her he'd had a one-night stand and was now having a baby. She'd leave him, and he couldn't bear to lose her from his life.

He knew he was being selfish, wanting both his wife and a relationship with his child. But he didn't know what else to do.

After a time, Andrea came to sit with him. "Her sister-in-law is here, so I left," she explained. "It would be weird to be in there when she had the baby. Especially since we work together."

Craig nodded. "I suppose it would."

"She was already halfway dilated by the time she arrived here," Andrea said. "If we'd gotten here any later, you would have been delivering a baby."

Craig raised his brows. "Or you."

Andrea shook her head. "No way. Not me. It would have had to be you."

An older couple came into the waiting room and sat, looking nervous. Craig thought the woman looked a little like Amanda. He took a chance.

"Are you Amanda's parents?" he asked.

They both nodded at once. "I'm Ronald DeCarlo," Ron said. "This is my wife, Rena. Do you work with Amanda?"

Craig stood and shook their hands. "I'm Craig Winslow. I own the agency she works at. This is Andrea Simms. She also works there. We brought Amanda to the hospital."

"It's so nice of you two to stay and wait," Rena said. "Amanda loves working at your office. She says everyone there is very nice to her."

"We really like her," Craig said. It seemed like an underwhelming thing to say about the woman having his baby, but he didn't know how else to express his feelings for her.

"She's amazing," Andrea said enthusiastically. "She studied and passed her test to become an agent faster than any of us. And she's so nice to work with."

Rena nodded. "That's my girl. She's a hard worker."

They all sat quietly again, watching the clock and waiting. Craig offered to get coffee and ran to the Starbucks down the street, bringing back coffee for everyone and cookies. After about an hour, a nurse in scrubs approached the group.

"Are any of you here for Amanda DeCarlo?" she asked, looking around.

Everyone stood up. The nurse laughed. "Okay. Maybe I should ask if any of you are related to her?"

"We're her parents," Ron said.

"Great. Amanda is doing fine, and so is the baby," the nurse said. "It was a fast delivery for a first baby. She may have to camp out at the hospital if she has another one."

"Can we see her?" Rena asked.

"Of course." She looked over at Craig and Andrea. "Maybe the parents could visit her first, and then you two can come in."

"That's fine," Craig said. "I'm just happy to hear all went well." He turned to the DeCarlos. "Congratulations on becoming grandparents."

Rena beamed. "It's our first. We're so happy."

"As you should be," Craig said, smiling.

After the DeCarlos left to visit Amanda, Craig slipped on his blazer and took out his car keys. "Now that we know Amanda and the baby are well, I think I'll head to my hotel."

"Don't you want to see the baby?" Andrea asked.

Craig wanted nothing more than to see the baby or even know if it was a boy or a girl. But he didn't belong here with family and friends. It might seem odd to everyone. "Send me a picture when you see the baby, and tell Amanda I'm so very happy for her."

"Okay. See you tomorrow," Andrea said.

Craig drove to the oceanside hotel he always stayed at and settled into his room. His thoughts were on Amanda the entire time. He went down to the restaurant and ate dinner while reading a book, then returned to his room. Craig almost texted Amanda to ask how she was doing, then stopped himself. That would be too personal for an employer to do.

His phone buzzed, and he picked it up off the nightstand. It was a message from Amanda with a photo.

"Say hello to our new baby boy," she'd written.

"A boy," Craig said softly, his heart filled with joy. He

studied the tiny peanut with big, dark eyes. He thought babies kept their eyes shut for the first few days, but this little guy was wide awake and raring to go.

"He's a keeper," he texted back. "Congratulations."

She sent back a smiley face. It was the most they could do without giving themselves away.

Craig knew he had a lifetime ahead of him of hiding his son. But it would be worth it to be able to be called Dad.

Chapter Thirteen

Amanda

Three days after giving birth, Amanda called Craig and asked if he'd like to come see the baby. He'd already returned to his Palos Verdes home for the weekend and had to wait until Monday. He told Marsha there was a problem at the Monterey office, so on Monday morning, he headed to Malibu to see his son.

And when he took the baby boy out of Amanda's arms and held him close, love poured out of him. He'd never known what he'd been missing out on until this moment.

"He's beautiful," Craig said, smiling widely. "He has your eyes," he told Amanda.

Amanda laughed. "His eyes will change. I think he looks a lot like you."

"Imagine that," he said. "Having a mini-me running around. I like the thought of it."

Amanda laughed.

"How are you feeling?" he asked her.

"I'm fine. I'm glad I can stay home for a while, though.

The baby only sleeps about three hours at a time, so I'm tired."
Amanda laughed. "My mom said she'd take off of work for a
month and stay with me, but I pleaded with her not to. I'm
enjoying my time alone with the baby. And this gives you a
chance to be around the baby, too, without any questions."

"Thank you," Craig said warmly. He rocked the baby side
to side in his arms. "Thank you for sharing him with me."

Amanda smiled. "I'm happy you can be a part of his life.
It might be an awkward situation, and it's a shame we have to
hide that he's yours, but we'll work it out as we go along."

He carried the baby over to the sofa and sat, watching the
baby sleep. He'd bought new furniture for Amanda when she'd
moved into the condo. And he'd helped her buy the furniture
for the baby's room as well. He didn't care how much everything cost. His baby meant more to him than anything else in
the world.

"I forgot," Craig said. "I haven't even asked you what you
named him."

Amanda smiled. "Remember that one evening we were the
only ones left at work, and we talked about names?"

Craig nodded.

"I decided to name the baby Maximilian after my grandfather. And his middle name is Michael."

Craig beamed. "My middle name! Thank you. That makes
me so happy."

"You're welcome," she said. "Of course, we'll just call him
Max for short. Maximilian is a big name for a little baby."

"I love it," Craig said.

As the weeks, then months, went by, Craig tried to see the
baby whenever he could. He gave Amanda money each month
to help with the baby's care. She protested at first, but when

she saw the enormous price of formula and diapers, she agreed.

Amanda worked from home the first three months after Max was born, then hired a babysitter to come to her home on weekdays to care for Max. Craig helped her with that expense, too. He told her it was the least he could do.

Every time Craig was in Malibu, he stopped by to see the baby. Amanda finally told him he should stay in the guest room so he could spend more time with Max. "After all, you pay for this place. Why not enjoy it?"

Craig hesitated at first but then gave in. "It would be nice to spend more time with Max," he said. "But any time you need me to stay at the hotel, just say so."

Amanda had no idea before having Max how much work it was to have a baby. But she also had never felt so much love for anyone else in her life. After only a few months, she couldn't imagine herself without the baby in her life.

A year after Max was born, Craig told Amanda he had a surprise for her. They both took Friday off from work, and he drove her and the baby up into the hills above Malibu. He pulled the car into a quiet neighborhood with nice homes that looked like they'd been built in the 1960s and 70s.

"Where exactly are we going?" Amanda asked, growing nervous. She trusted Craig completely, but she was afraid he was going to introduce them to friends and blow their cover.

"Hopefully, home," Craig said, giving her a sideways glance, then smiling.

He pulled up into the driveway of a nice-looking ranch-style house with a large lawn in front and a double garage.

"Come on," he said, getting out of the car. He ran around to the other side and opened Amanda's door—always the gentleman—and then unhooked the baby from the car seat in the back.

"Why are we here?" Amanda asked, glancing around.

"Just look at that view," Craig said, turning toward the street. The houses on the opposite side of the street were built lower so as not to block the view.

"Oh, my goodness. It's beautiful!" Amanda said. Spread out in front of her was the Pacific Ocean.

Craig smiled. "Wouldn't that be nice to wake up to every day?"

"Dream on," Amanda said.

Craig waved for her to follow him, and they walked up the path to the front door. Balancing Max in his right arm, he pulled a key out of his pants pocket and unlocked the door.

"What are you doing?" Amanda asked. She looked around, wondering if they were going to get in trouble for entering someone else's house.

"Come on in," Craig said excitedly. He walked ahead of her, and Amanda had no other option but to follow.

The house was beautiful. A big picture window in the living room looked out to the view of the ocean. There was a Spanish-style fireplace in the corner and a beautiful sofa on the opposite wall. Past the entryway, Amanda saw a dining room with a large table and chairs and the kitchen beyond.

"This house has two bedrooms and two bathrooms," Craig said, setting Max down on the living room floor. Max wasn't walking quite yet but still managed to get around quickly so they always had to keep an eye on him. "And the backyard is to die for. Come look."

Amanda closed the front door so Max wouldn't escape and followed Craig into the dining room. Out the back window was a huge backyard that was surrounded by trees and tall bushes, making it very private.

"A person could easily add a pool and still have a lot of yard left. We could even put a swing set and jungle gym right over there for Max," Craig said.

"We?" Amanda turned and stared at Craig. "Did you buy this house?"

Craig nodded. "I did. Please hear me out before you say no."

"No," Amanda said, turning back to the living room.

"Amanda. Please." Craig followed her. "Max is growing so fast. He needs a yard and a nice neighborhood to grow up in. Wouldn't it be nice in a couple of years to be able to stand at the kitchen window and watch him play safely in his own yard?"

Amanda spun on her heel and faced Craig. Out of the corner of her eye, she saw that Max was walking with the aid of the coffee table. He was growing up fast. "I can't take a house from you, Craig," she said. "You've been generous enough to pay my rent at the condo. At some point, I need to take care of myself and Max, and I certainly can't afford to take care of this house."

"You don't have to pay for the house," Craig said. "I own it. You can live here as long as you like. And it's not charity. I bought this house for investment purposes. It was run down and needed fixing up, so I got a good price on it and had it remodeled. That's why everything looks new."

"But it's still your house, Craig," Amanda said. "I can't keep taking things from you."

"You'd be doing me a favor," Craig said. "Honestly. If I keep this house, let's say, for ten years, its value will skyrocket like everything else in Malibu. You and Max can live here rent-free until I decide I need to sell it. Think about it, Amanda. It's better than wasting money on rent."

Amanda walked over to the sofa near Max and scooped him up into her lap. She appreciated everything Craig had done for her, but this seemed too extravagant. They weren't in any kind of physical relationship. They were just friends who happened to have a baby together. Wouldn't it be wrong of her to live in a house he owned?

Craig came to sit beside them. "Please use the house," he said. "It's a great place for Max to grow up. You have a short walk or drive down to the beach below, where he can play. I want you and Max to have the best of everything."

Amanda looked up and saw the gorgeous view out the window. This was a dream house. She'd never be able to buy something like this on her own. "I don't know, Craig," she said. "Yes, it's a beautiful home in a lovely area. And yes, I want the best for Max. But it feels wrong."

Craig sat back and chuckled. "Everything we're doing is all new territory for both of us. But if you put it down to the basics, you're Max's mother, and I'm his father. If I can give you two a good life, why shouldn't I?"

Yes. Their situation wasn't easy in any way. But it had worked so far. And Amanda had to admit paying for a house made more sense than paying rent.

"If I say yes and live here, then you have to at least let me pay the utility bills," Amanda said, feeling herself giving in.

"I'll be happy to let you pay the utility bills," Craig said.

"And what if, at some point, I start dating someone seriously? How does that work if you own the house?" Amanda asked.

Craig smiled. "I may own the house, but I don't own you. Of course, you'll start dating again. I'm not going to try to stop you from having a life. As long as I can have some kind of relationship with Max, that's all I ask."

Max was squirming in her lap, so Amanda put him down. He grabbed ahold of Craig's knee and smiled up at his father. Craig smiled back as the little boy moved slowly along the couch to the end table.

Amanda sighed. Max definitely needed his father. There was no doubt in her mind that Craig adored Max and would always make sure he was taken care of.

"Okay. I give in," Amanda said, lifting her arms in a sign of surrender. "But I'm not sure how I'll explain owning a house in Malibu to everyone at work."

Craig grinned. "Just tell them you're renting it from a friend. They won't even question it."

Amanda stood and walked through the dining room to the kitchen. Everything from the cabinets to the appliances here was brand new. It was the perfect house.

"Hey, big guy. Let's go see your room," Craig said, lifting Max up in the air and spinning him around. The little boy squealed with delight as Craig carried him to the back bedroom.

Amanda stared out the kitchen window to the backyard. Yes, a sandbox, a jungle gym, and a swing set would look great out there. She smiled. Despite what she'd said to Craig, she couldn't help but be excited about moving into this house.

Chapter Fourteen

Amanda

Today

Amanda was exhausted. After she'd dropped Max off at school, she'd gone to every listing of apartments, condos, and houses to rent, and each one was worse than the last. She had less than a month to move out of Craig's house, and she had no idea where to go.

She had to be close enough to the office for work and wanted Max to continue attending his current school. But everything around the area was expensive, and there wasn't much to rent. Since the fires in Malibu and Pacific Palisades, the price of rent had gone up and there were fewer places left. She'd been lucky that her home had been spared from the fire. In fact, most of her neighborhood had been spared by some miracle. During the fires, she'd evacuated to her mother's house in Torrance until she was able to return to the house. Aside from the smell of smoke, the house was fine.

But now she had to leave the only house Max had ever known.

She couldn't blame Craig's wife. Not at all. She knew Marsha had misinterpreted her and Craig's relationship, but would it matter to her if she knew the truth? She'd still kick her out of the house. And since the house still had a mortgage on it, she couldn't blame her for wanting to sell it.

She and Craig had spoken many times throughout the years about the cost of the house and how it was affecting his financial situation. Craig never complained, but Amanda suspected he'd overextended himself. First, he sold the Monterey office to his employees, then he sold the Malibu office. He'd offered to pay her share of the buyout so she could be an owner, too, but she'd declined. Amanda had taken so much from Craig already. She couldn't let him give her a piece of the business he'd built from the ground up.

Amanda wished she'd been stronger and had flatly refused to live in the Malibu house. She'd be in a better situation now if she had. But he'd worn her down—always saying it was for Max. And while she also wanted to give Max the best life possible, she should have made sure it was affordable for her if anything happened to Craig.

Tears filled her eyes as she sat in traffic on Highway One. She had adored Craig. She was never in love with him, and they didn't have a physical relationship, but he was so kind and generous to both her and Max. Sometimes, when he came to Malibu, he'd stay at the house, and they'd take Max to the beach, or he'd play games with the young boy. He'd spent as much time as possible with Max, and for that, Amanda would be forever grateful. Unfortunately, Craig hadn't made a plan for her and Max in the event that he should die.

But then again, why would she have expected him to? He'd paid for her house and all she'd had to pay for were the utilities.

Because of that, she'd been able to put aside a nice nest egg for herself and Max. She earned a nice living, too, all thanks to Craig's encouragement. But California, and especially places like Malibu, were so expensive. And she didn't want to spend all her savings and have nothing left.

The day Amanda saw Marsha at the cemetery had been difficult. While she'd love to be able to explain her relationship with Craig, she could tell immediately that Marsha wasn't ready to listen. Again, she couldn't blame her for that. But that conversation was ingrained in her mind and wouldn't go away.

The necklace. The pretty gold heart with the diamonds on it. Craig had given that to her five years ago, too, on Mother's Day. He'd thanked her for giving him the greatest gift of all— Max. It hadn't been a gift given out of love for her but out of his love for his son. Until that day at the cemetery, Amanda hadn't known that Marsha had the same necklace. Amanda could see how she'd misinterpret it, seeing it on her. Amanda had cherished the lovely necklace, but now, she felt bad wearing it.

All of this was tearing her up inside.

Amanda pointed her car towards Max's elementary school. She'd take another day off work tomorrow and continue to search for a place to live. She was starting all over again. Even the furniture wasn't hers. But she told herself it didn't matter. Max had a father for the first nine years of his life, and it was worth all the trouble it caused her now. Because Max wouldn't remember where they lived as much as he'd remember the man he'd called Dad. And that was all that mattered.

Chapter Fifteen

Marsha

Marsha stayed at the inn for two more days, enjoying her walks on the beach and thinking deeply about her life. Her head was clearer, and she felt lighter than she had when she'd arrived. She knew it would take time to fix the mess Craig had left her, and she was finally ready to do the hard work of moving on with her life.

It was time to go home.

The morning she left, she thanked Joanna and Melinda for being such wonderful hosts. "I'm sure this won't be the last time I come here," she told them. "And please send me a notice when you get married, Melinda. I'd love to send you a gift."

Melinda promised she would and Marsha left the inn in a much happier frame of mind.

She'd already said her goodbyes to Andrew Trelow, who'd left early in the morning the day before. And she thanked the older man for sharing his story. "You've given me something to think about," she told him as she hugged him. "I think it was fate that we met."

"Or maybe Irene had something to do with it," Andrew said, winking.

Marsha laughed but didn't discount what he'd said. God worked in mysterious ways, and who was she to question it.

As she pulled out of the parking lot onto the highway, she called Kristi. "I'm coming home," she told her friend. "I'll be at the gallery tomorrow morning, and we can start working on making the gallery profitable."

"That's great," Kristi said. "Are you feeling better?"

"Yes," Marsha said with a long, relieved sigh. "Much better. I think I'm ready to make some big decisions about my life. I'll see you tomorrow."

Three hours later, she pulled into the driveway of her Palos Verdes home and sighed. It was nice to be home, even with all the memories attached to it. Taking her suitcase from the trunk, she walked inside, set her suitcase down, and walked directly to the large picture window. That view! Even though she'd spent time near the ocean these past few days, it still wasn't like her view here. This view was familiar. It belonged to her.

The next day, Marsha walked into the gallery, and before putting her things in the back room, she hugged Kristi tightly. "I'm sorry I worried you this past week. So much has happened, and I had to clear my head. I feel so much better now."

"I'm glad you're doing better," Kristi said, hugging her friend back.

They got right down to work, discussing ways to make the most out of the gallery. Both women loved owning it and wanted to make it profitable.

"The first thing we have to do is change the percentage we charge for housing the artists' work," Marsha said. "I know it will be hard since we've become friends with our artists, but it's necessary. We've been working with them on a 50/50 basis. But we need to change that to 60/40."

Kristi's eyes grew wide. "I know a few who won't like that."

"I know," Marsha said, nodding in agreement. "But all the other local gift shops and galleries charge that much, and most of them demand exclusivity. We don't ask the artists to be exclusive with us. And if they feel forty percent is too low, they can always raise the price to earn it back."

"I'm not looking forward to those phone calls," Kristi said.

"It will be hard, but let's put it this way. Either we get a higher percentage, or we close our doors. That's the honest truth."

They also talked about adding some movable wall panels to create more space to hang paintings. The more items they had for sale, hopefully, the more they'd sell.

After they'd decided on a plan to change the gallery, Marsha made a few personal phone calls. She called her accountant and asked if he'd talked to the Torrance insurance office about the employees purchasing it. He said he had and told her the price they were willing to pay.

"It's a good offer," Tom said. "And since I know how much that office earns, I think it's a good buyout. But, of course, it's up to you."

"Sell it," Marsha said. "Send the information to my lawyer, and he can draw up the paperwork."

"I'll get right on that," Tom said. "How are you doing?"

"I'm fine," Marsha told him. "I took a few days off to clear my head, and now I'm ready to take care of things."

"Great. I'll call Richard and let him know you're selling the office." Tom hesitated. "Just so you know, the monthly mortgage payment for the Malibu house comes due at the end of the month. I've always paid it for Craig. Should I continue?"

Marsha sighed. More money she had to spend that she couldn't afford. "Yes. Go ahead. We're putting it up for sale next month. Could you send me a total of what's left on the mortgage? Then I'll know what profit I'll make off it."

"Certainly," Tom said. "I'm sure you'll make a nice profit off that house."

That evening, as Marsha sat in her dining room, eating a frozen dinner, she wondered if this would be her life from now on. Once all her finances were taken care of and the Malibu house was out of her hair, what else was ahead for her? Would she spend the next thirty or forty years alone, rambling around in this house? She loved her house on the cliff and the large yard. But it was just her now. And the taxes were high, as well as the insurance. Could she even afford to keep it for the rest of her life?

She knew that Craig hadn't left anything for Amanda and Max. She'd asked the accountant specifically about where the money from the sale of the businesses had gone, and he'd assured her all the money had gone toward everyday living expenses. Clothes, jewelry, cruises, vacations, and nice cars. And, of course, the upkeep of this house. Did she really want to spend the rest of her years on this planet buying things and taking care of this home?

It surprised her that she was even thinking this way.

As she crawled into bed that night, she couldn't stop thinking about Craig's mistress and son. He'd left them nothing to live on in the event of his death. Nothing. The house wasn't in Amanda's name, and he hadn't given her big chunks of money. When Amanda leaves the Malibu house, she'll have nothing except her job and her son. A week ago, Marsha would have thought the woman deserved to be left with nothing. Now, that thought didn't sit well with her.

The next day, she called Craig's brother, Jeffrey.

"Marsha!" he said, sounding happy to hear from her. "What can I do for you."

"First of all," Marsha said. "I'm sorry I got angry with you about knowing about the Malibu house and, well, you know. It wasn't your fault. I had no one else to express my frustration to since I couldn't yell at Craig."

"Honestly, I didn't blame you for being angry. Craig put me in a tough position, but I didn't want to be the one to tell you about the situation. I'm so sorry," Jeffery said.

"It was Craig's mess, not yours," Marsha said. "And I'm the one left to clean it up. But enough of that. I have a favor to ask of you."

"Anything," he said.

"Will you keep your eye out for a place I could buy, maybe in my neighborhood or nearby, where I have less house and less land to deal with but also still have a view?"

"You want to move?" Jeffrey sounded shocked.

"Only if it's the right place. I can't see myself staying in that expensive house for however many years I have left on this earth," Marsha said. "I think it's time for a change."

"I'm happy to look for a place for you," Jeffrey said. "But you know, they say you shouldn't make any big changes for at least a year after losing a spouse."

Marsha laughed. "After everything I've been through since Craig died, looking for a new place is the least of my problems. I think I'm making a smart decision."

"Okay. I'll be on the lookout," Jeffrey said. "I'm glad to hear you're doing better. Kristi tells me there will be a few changes at the gallery as well."

"Yes. But they are all for the better," Marsha said. "And if I'd known it wasn't profitable these past five years, I would have implemented changes a long time ago. I know Craig thought he was protecting me from bad news, but honesty is always better to just tell the truth."

"I agree," Jeffrey said.

"Also, there's one more thing I need you to do," Marsha said. She explained her idea to him, and again, his voice sounded stunned.

"Are you sure?" Jeffrey asked.

"Yes," Marsha said. "It has to be done."

Marsha smiled as she hung up. For the first time since learning about all the lies that Craig had told her, she actually felt better. Relieved, even. She knew what she was about to do was the right thing.

The next week was a busy blur for Marsha. She called a company that sold gallery walls and purchased three movable walls that they delivered right away. She and Kristi put them together themselves because they didn't want to pay extra for someone else to do it. They had also made the calls to their artists to tell them the new percentage. They made an exception for the items already in the store for sale, but any new items would go under the new percentage. Some balked, and one person came in and took their photos off the wall. But most of them agreed it was fair. Other galleries were charging that same percentage, so it didn't surprise them.

"And I want you to stay in business," Marco told Marsha when she talked to him. "You sell more of my sculptures than any other gallery. If I left you, I'd be a starving artist."

Marsha appreciated that he felt that way. She wanted to be fair, but she needed to make a profit, too.

At Marsha's request, their artists brought more paintings, photos, and sculptures into the shop to sell. When they saw the idea of adding more walls for hanging space, they all complimented Kristi and Marsha on it. "We'll sell more, and you'll make more money," one artist said. "It's a win-win situation."

Marsha hoped that would be true.

Marsha also spent time with Jeffrey to see several homes and condos for sale. She hadn't found the perfect place yet, but she knew she would. It was just a matter of time.

By the end of the week, Marsha was exhausted. She spent the weekend at home, going through clothing and personal items, deciding what to keep and what to give away or sell. They had ten years worth of items sitting in the house and she didn't need to bring it all to wherever she decided to move.

When she'd packed up Craig's suits, shirts, and other clothing a couple of weeks ago, she'd been angry. Now, she was more sentimental about what she kept and what she was giving away. She knew he hadn't planned to die so soon, and she thought he might have fixed their financial situation by the time they retired. But she also knew he never planned on telling her about his other life. About his son. And that hurt.

But Andrew Trelow was right. As she packed away memories, she realized there were so many happy ones to cherish. And she wanted to remember those good times despite all that happened since. Because no one could take away their twenty years of happiness, even if it wasn't built on complete honesty. Hopefully, as time went on, she'd forget his betrayal and only remember the good times. She could only hope.

Chapter Sixteen

Marsha

On the last day of the month, Marsha had one last thing to do to fix Craig's mess. She took the day off from the gallery, got into her car, and drove north on Highway One. Despite Jeffrey telling her she could let someone else handle this, she had to do it herself. Marsha knew people would judge her for what she was about to do or tell her she was crazy, but she didn't care. It was something that had to be done.

Once she was in Malibu, she took the winding road up into the hills and pulled into the peaceful neighborhood. Parking on the street, Marsha picked up the large manila envelope sitting on the passenger seat, took a deep breath, and walked up the sidewalk to the front door.

Knocking once, she waited. Marsha hadn't called ahead, so there was a possibility that no one was home. But Marsha knew where she worked and could take the envelope to her there if necessary.

The door opened, and the woman on the other side looked stunned to see Marsha standing there.

"Hello, Amanda. Can we talk for a moment?" Marsha asked steadily.

Amanda opened the door wider. "Yes. Of course." She moved out of the way to let Marsha walk inside. Instead, Marsha stood in the doorway, gazing inside the house.

"You haven't moved any of your furniture yet," Marsha said, surprised.

"I know I'm supposed to move out by today, and I'm trying to pack what I can," Amanda said apologetically. "I spoke to your lawyer, and he said I could have a few extra days. It's been difficult finding a new place I can afford."

Marsha studied her face for a moment and was about to speak when Amanda rushed on.

"Besides. The furniture isn't mine. It all belonged to Craig. I'm only taking our personal items with us."

Marsha wasn't surprised. Craig would have taken care of everything for Amanda and her son. That was who he was. "It's your furniture now," Marsha said. "I have no interest in taking anything from this house."

"Oh," Amanda said softly. "Thank you."

"I just came here today to give you this," Marsha said, handing her the thick envelope.

Amanda frowned as she stared at it. "What is it?"

"I know Craig didn't leave you anything in his will or give you any money to take care of his son in the event he died. And that was wrong," Marsha said. "So, I signed over this house to you. It's yours to do whatever you want with. Keep it, sell it, whatever."

Amanda's mouth dropped open. "Really?"

Marsha remained stoic. "Yes. Granted, there's still a mortgage on it, but there's also a lot of equity in the house. If you sell, you should be able to afford a nice home for you and your son and have some left over. I've paid this month's mortgage payment. You'll be responsible for it from now on. You'll need to stop by my lawyer's office to finish filling out the paperwork in that envelope, but then it will be yours."

Tears filled Amanda's eyes. "Thank you so much. I didn't know how I would be able to pay for another place. This is so generous of you."

"You're welcome," Marsha said, her voice kinder. "Just promise me you'll take good care of Craig's son. As Craig would have wanted you to."

"Absolutely," Amanda said, wiping her eyes. "He's the joy of my life."

Marsha nodded, then turned to leave.

"Wait!" Amanda called after her. "Do you have time to come inside and talk? I'd really like you to know something important."

Marsha doubted that this woman could tell her anything she'd want to know. She turned back toward Amanda. "No. Thank you. I'd better leave before I change my mind and take that envelope back. I wish you well." She turned and hurried to her car. As she slid into the driver's seat, she heard Amanda call out, "God bless you."

Marsha wasn't sure if God even cared about her anymore. But she'd done the right thing; she knew that in her heart. And as she drove down Highway One toward her Palos Verdes home, she felt like a heavy weight had been lifted from her shoulders.

As the weeks went by, the pain Marsha felt over Craig's betrayal faded. She was too busy looking for a new place to live and working at the gallery to dwell on it. She knew Amanda had gone to Richard to finalize the transfer of the Malibu house into her name. Marsha had also put Jeffrey's card in the envelope, and Amanda had hired him to sell the house for her.

Jeffrey had been shocked when he'd heard that Marsha had given the young woman the house. He'd called Marsha and told her that it was a kind, selfless thing to do.

"It's what Craig would have wanted," Marsha told him. Because despite everything, she wanted to do what was right.

A month after talking to Amanda, Marsha was working on invoices at the gallery when Kristi walked in with the mail.

"I saw the postman when I went for coffee," Kristi said, handing a coffee to Marsha and setting the mail down. "There's a letter here for you." She lifted her eyes to meet Marsha's eyes. "It's from Amanda."

Marsha stopped working and stared at the plain white envelope. The last thing she wanted to do was read what that woman had to say. She was working at putting everything behind her and didn't need a reminder of the one thing that had hurt her so deeply.

"Toss it on the desk in the back, please," Marsha said, going back to her invoices. "I'll read it another time."

Kristi knew about Marsha giving away the house and that Jeffrey was selling it for Amanda. "Aren't you curious about what she has to say?"

Marsha sighed. "No. Not really. It just brings up too many painful memories."

Kristi nodded her understanding and took the mail to the back room.

That night, after arriving home, Marsha gazed around her home. She'd done a good job of trimming down the excess in the house. She had her furniture, of course, but she got rid of anything that didn't bring her joy. Her closet was less crowded, too. She'd given away clothing she hadn't worn in a while and so many pairs of shoes she knew she'd never wear again. It felt good to purge. If she found the right place to move into, she'd start over without clutter or junk.

Only two months had gone by since losing Craig, yet it felt like he'd been gone for a lifetime. Her life had changed in so many ways since the accident. She worked longer hours at the gallery, yet didn't mind it. And even though she loved this house, she was looking forward to buying a new place and making it her own.

She also got tired of frozen dinners. Now, she planned ahead for meals and ate mostly fresh foods like salads with grilled chicken or shrimp and pasta meals. She'd become quite adept at using the gas grill, and it tasted so much better than the frozen stuff.

Tonight, she grilled a small piece of salmon and pulled out the large bucket of salad she kept in her fridge. She sat at the table, even though it was dark outside and she couldn't see the ocean. But she could hear it, and she was soothed by the sound.

As she ate, she thought about the letter Amanda sent her. She hadn't opened it at the gallery and wasn't sure if she'd open it at all. But Kristi had been right. She was a little curious about what the young woman had written. She doubted, though, that anything she wrote would make Marsha feel better about Craig's betrayal.

After eating, she placed the dishes in the dishwasher and changed into night clothes. Passing her purse in the bedroom, Marsha saw the letter sticking out of it. With a sigh, she lifted the envelope from her purse, went out to her living room, and sat on the sofa. She guessed it wouldn't hurt to at least read it.

Opening the envelope, she pulled the handwritten pages out, surprised at how many there were. Steeling herself, she opened the pages and read the script.

Dear Mrs. Winslow,

I hope you decide to read my letter. I couldn't live with myself if you went through the rest of your life not knowing the truth. First, thank you for giving me the house. You can't imagine what a difference it will make in my life and my son's. I have it up for sale and am searching for a less expensive place. Craig was very generous, allowing me to live there for free all these years, even when I fought him on it at first. But it was such a lovely place to raise Max that it was hard to say a firm no.

I want you to know that Craig and I did not have an intimate relationship. We only had one (intoxicated) night together, and we both regretted our actions immediately afterward. Craig loved you so much and was scared to hurt you and lose you. Neither of us wanted a relationship in the way I think you believe we had. We were co-workers and friends. He was a kind, thoughtful, and caring man. But all his love was for you alone.

Max was the result of that single night, and from the moment I told Craig, he was supportive. He offered to do whatever was necessary to help me with Max. Every step of the way, I told him he didn't have to do anything, but he insisted. When he showed me the house a year after Max was born, I refused it. But as I said, it was hard to say no to Craig. So, I lived there and he'd come to visit while he was in town. But our relationship was completely platonic. He just wanted to be a part of Max's life, and I wanted that for my son. I never meant for you to be hurt by it, and I'm so sorry.

As for the necklace, it was not given as a token of love for me.

Craig gave it to me one Mother's Day as a token of gratitude for allowing him to have Max in his life. While I agree it was a bad choice for him to give you and me the exact same necklace, I can only say he meant well. I hope you can forgive him for that.

I also hope you can forgive Craig for our one night together. He never meant to hurt you, nor did I. Even the most perfect people can make mistakes. But at least that mistake brought Max to me, and he will live on as a reminder of Craig, who was the kindest man I've ever met.

I wish you nothing but the best in the future, and thank you again for making the future better for both me and my son.

Sincerely,
Amanda

Marsha stared at the letter for a long time. Was it true? Or was Amanda lying to make her feel better? Then again, why would Amanda lie? Marsha had already given her the house, so there was no reason to lie about their relationship.

If what Amanda wrote was true, Marsha would be able to forgive Craig. Yes, he'd had a one-night stand, which was so out of character for him. But he'd taken responsibility for his actions and took care of his son. Marsha had to give him credit for that.

She stood, walked to her bedroom, and opened her jewelry box. Lying there was the heart necklace. She lifted it from the box and stared at it for a long time as tears filled her eyes. She'd loved the gift so much. Now that she knew the truth about the necklace, she thought that maybe she could love it again.

"Oh, Craig," she said softly.

Marsha sat on the bed and wiped away her tears. She wondered if she would have been able to forgive him if she'd known about the one-night affair all those years ago. She didn't know the answer to that, and she realized it didn't matter anymore. Craig was gone. As Andrew Trelow would say, it all came down to the heart of the matter. Craig had been an attentive, hardworking, and loving husband. Even with his one mistake, he'd been a good man.

Marsha thought she could live with that.

Chapter Seventeen

Marsha

One Year Later

The gallery had been busy all morning and neither Kristi nor Marsha had stopped for a break. At noon, Marsha told Kristi to go eat lunch, and by one, Marsha headed over to the coffee shop to grab a coffee and maybe a snack.

It was a lovely fall day—not too hot but warm, with a nice breeze coming off the ocean. She smiled as she walked, thankful for everything in her life these days. The gallery was making a nice profit, and eight months ago, she'd sold her house and moved into a lovely two-bedroom, two-bathroom condo with a balcony and a view of the ocean. She loved her new place. It suited her busy life because she no longer had to worry about the upkeep of the house or the grounds.

The coffee shop was busy when she walked in, so she found the end of the line and waited. A tall man with sandy blond hair came to stand behind her.

"Mrs. Winslow?" the man asked.

Marsha turned and looked up at the man. She wasn't sure

who it was, but he did look familiar.

"Sorry. Of course, you don't remember me. I'm Officer Mike Becker. I was the one who drove you home that night."

Marsha deflated. "Oh, my goodness. How embarrassing. You must think I'm a nut case."

He chuckled. "Not at all. You were going through the grief process. We all do strange things when we're grieving."

Marsha studied him. He'd been in uniform, and it had been dark out that night, so she hadn't really had a good look at him. Plus, she'd been crying. Today, though, he looked handsome with sandy blond hair and deep blue eyes. And he was dressed casually in jeans and a cotton shirt. "I doubt if you've ever fallen to pieces in your life," she said.

"Me? Oh, don't be so sure." He smiled. "I stopped by your house a couple of times the week after your incident to check on you, but no one answered. I figured you had gone away for a while."

Marsha was surprised. "You checked up on me?"

"Sure. You seemed so sad. I just wanted to make sure you were okay," Mike said.

"Well, that was very nice of you," Marsha said. "I did go away for a few days to clear my head. A lot was going on at that time."

"So, is your head clear now?" he asked, smiling.

Marsha laughed. "Clearer."

Marsha was the next in line and when she stepped up to order, Mike spoke up. "Let me buy your coffee," he offered.

Marsha hesitated but then nodded. "I want a muffin, too," she said.

"Absolutely," Mike told her.

Once their order came, he asked if she'd like to sit for a

while and talk. She agreed, and they found a table outside under an umbrella.

"What brings you out here today?" Marsha asked after sipping her coffee.

"Ugh!" Mike said, then laughed. "I'm shopping for a present for my baby sister's fortieth birthday, and I have no idea what she'd like. Her husband is giving her a big party."

"Well, I know of a charming little gallery a few steps from here where you could find a nice gift," Marsha said.

"It must be a good place if you're recommending it," Mike said.

"I'm one of the owners there, so I have to say it's an amazing place," she said, grinning.

"Really. I didn't know that. I guess I'd better go in and look then, although I'm sure it's too fancy for a guy on a police officer's salary."

"Maybe not if you have the right connections," Marsha said with a wink.

He laughed, and they talked for over an hour.

"I'd better get back to the gallery before Kristi thinks I got lost," Marsha said. "Thank you for the coffee and muffin."

"My pleasure." He hesitated, then asked, "Would you want to go out for dinner with me tonight? And if you think my asking is completely out of line, please tell me to shove off."

Marsha couldn't help but laugh. She liked Mike Becker. He seemed like a nice man. "I'd love to have dinner with you tonight."

He smiled broadly. "Wonderful."

"We can decide where while I help you choose a gift for your sister," Marsha said.

He laughed. "It's a deal."

As they walked together toward the gallery, Marsha felt happiness welling up inside her. She'd always love Craig, there was no doubt. But maybe it was time for her to find happiness again. It could be with Mike Becker or someone else. She was open to whatever came her way.

-End-

About the Author

Deanna Lynn Sletten is the author of THE LAST LADY OF THE SILVER SCREEN, MRS. WINCHESTER'S BIOGRAPHER, THE ONES WE LEAVE BEHIND, THE WOMEN OF GREAT HERON LAKE, FINDING LIBBIE, MAGGIE'S TURN, and several other titles. She writes heartwarming women's fiction, captivating historical fiction, a murder mystery series, and romance novels with unforgettable characters. She has also written one middle-grade novel that takes you on the adventure of a lifetime.

Deanna is married and has two grown children. When not writing, she enjoys peaceful walks in the woods around her property with her beautiful Australian Shepherd, traveling, photography, and relaxing on the lake.

Deanna loves hearing from her readers. Visit her website at: deannalsletten.com